THE REST OF THE WORLD

THE REST OF THE WORLD

Stories

Adam Schwartz

Washington Writers' Publishing House
Washington, DC

COVER DESIGN by Lou Ann Robinson
BOOK DESIGN and TYPESETTING by Barbara Shaw

Library of Congress Cataloging-in-Publication Data

Names: Schwartz, Adam, 1965 February 1- author.
Title: The rest of the world : stories / Adam Schwartz.
Description: First. | Washington, DC : Washington Writers Publishing House,
   [2020] | Summary: "The heroes in this acclaimed story collection are kids coming of age in a Baltimore that owes them better. They are studies of characters in crisis—delivered by a writer whose empathies illuminate the longings of teens and young adults forced to navigate complex moral choices. These characters betray one another, seek redemption, rescue loved ones, plot hustles, and refuse to give up on themselves or each other."— Provided by publisher.

Printed in the United States of America

WASHINGTON WRITERS' PUBLISHING HOUSE
P. O. Box 15271
Washington, D.C. 20003
More information: www.washingtonwriters.org

CONTENTS

These stories first appeared or are forthcoming in the following publications:

"Carmen and Ant" was a finalist in *Narrative*'s fall 2017 contest, a finalist in *New Letters* 2018 Prize for Fiction and will appear in *Raritan* (Winter 2021)

"Wizzur" will appear in *Gargoyle* (Fall 2020)

"Pretty Girls" appeared in *Mississippi Review* (Summer 2015)

"Pavane for a Dead Princess" appeared in *december Magazine* (Spring 2016)

"U.S. History" appeared in *The Doctor T.J. Eckleburg Review* (June 2016)

"Elegance" appeared in *Saranac Review* (Fall 2017)

"The Rest of the World" won *Poets & Writers'* 2012 WEX Award and *Philadelphia Stories'* 2012 Marguerite McGlinn contest. The story was also anthologized in *The Best of Philadelphia Stories, 10th Anniversary Edition.*

"What Is Gravity?" was first published in *Arkansas Review* (Spring 1997) and also won *Baltimore City Paper*'s 1999 story contest.

FOR MY LADY

And for my mother and father—
wonderful seekers who cared deeply about
people and ideas and who told me stories.

Want of courage is the last offense to be pardoned by young men.

—Alexander Pushkin, "The Shot"

Things seldom end in one event.

—Richard Ford, "Great Falls"

If there is hope for this world, it is in our ability to see ourselves in others, in persons who do not look like us, do not talk like us, do not live like us, but who in every essential way is exactly like us.

—Elizabeth Nunez, *Boundaries*

PAVANE FOR A DEAD PRINCESS

think of that time, before everything got crazy, and I see Missy Ha like she was then: nineteen with a heart-shaped face, teeth like fine china, and a little girl's giggle for something she knew that you didn't. Other girls tried so hard to make themselves look cute. Missy was pretty just because. And in that smile that stayed in her eyes, you thought you might see something better in yourself.

They were Koreans, her family, with a carry-out up the hill. You'd see their neon wok throwing off samurai blades of sunshine, blinking out the words *Democratic Best* before you even got there. The Has, most of them anyway, lived in the neighborhood, either above the store or next door. When you stepped up to order your food, the Has weren't hiding behind some plexiglass cocoon, buzzing their own in and out. They took your order like real people. Face-to-face, talking about whatever—the sewer grate at the curb puffing rotten eggs again or how nobody's giving Obama a chance or that crazy *2012* movie that had some people so shook you couldn't tell them it was made up.

Summers, the Has hosed off their front sidewalks and eased hustlers off their corners and chilled outside on the sidewalk, reading Korean newspapers, ooh'ing and ah'ing over someone's new baby and always tidying their roses. The Has did a lot for those roses: gave 'em bone meal and lime, spritz from a mister, nailed little wooden slats into the brick to help them climb, then talked those vines halfway up the front of the house.

Every June they hosted a block party where they cooked out for the whole neighborhood: hamburgers, hotdogs, lemons stuck through with peppermint sticks, and even short ribs if you went early enough. You'd smell the charcoal meat for blocks, and you knew it was summer. In the fall, Sundays especially, they represented in purple Ravens jerseys, just like a lot of people. The one they call Unc, with the spiky hair, might even cross the street and take a rip of whatever was going around—Henny or Grey Goose—and then lose a few dollars playing spades in his checkered-trim chef's shirt. Everyone liked the Has. They were good people, like I said, real people.

But none of what I've told here meant they wanted Missy mixing with the customers. And that's what I was, a customer. Regular enough they even called me by my favorite order: Number Five, for the spicy yakami.

Everything changed after Ma Ha caught Missy showing me her book of drawings. We were low on the back steps, and the big spiral lay in my lap. She kept reaching across my side to flip the pages, embarrassed for me to look too hard. My heart jumped each time she pressed against me, snug.

Missy's drawings were wild. They were on thick paper, some in rubbed charcoal, others she'd painted freehand in peaches and grays that had crinkled the edges. Lines might be twine-thin or much bolder. The people in them wore open leather vests, mesh garters, push-ups, bustiers. A couple of the chicks even had their titties out.

Jealousy's a nasty feeling—starts eating you up even when it's got no call. And I could feel my face getting hot because you wouldn't think Missy was that kind of girl.

She saw my pinched eyes and flipped the page. But the next page was just as crowded with other half-naked people.

I took off my baseball cap and stroked my hair forward. "What kind of parties you been going to?"

She cringed, scrunching up her shoulders, then palmed back a giggle.

"Something funny?" I asked.

All of the smothered laughter just went into her eyes.

I was about to say something really crude. "Whatever."

She rocked forward, caught herself and came up laughing. "They're not real, Bahia."

I rapped a knuckle on the page. "They must've come from somewhere."

"Relax," she said, her smile fading. "They're only in my head."

The kitchen fan was softly venting out, its blades a ghosty whirl of sooty vinegar blowing through the alley.

"Don't you believe me?" she asked.

"They don't look like nobody's strangers to me." I started redoing the laces on my tennis. "They look real. Like true blue people."

"No, sweetie." She slipped a gentle hand behind my neck. "It's art."

"Art?"

"Yes," she said. "Made up."

"Oh," I said, unsure if this made it better. Then, turning a page, I realized there *was* something off in the way she'd drawn these people, some faraway look in their faces, like how manikins got their feelings missing.

"But these kinda dirty, aren't they?" I asked.

"Like obscene?"

"Like someone might think you easy-peazy."

She dropped her eyes and looked away. "Just 'cause I stay inside doesn't mean I'm boring."

I turned another page, starting to feel dumb for getting heated. "Why do you draw this stuff anyway?"

She did not answer right away. "I shouldn't have brought them out here."

We were quiet and it's hard to explain because it's been a while now, but I still wonder about those pictures and the sad feeling they gave off and what those lost, oval faces were looking for.

Then Ma Ha stepped out, cracked an old mop handle against the iron railing and called sharply in Korean. I felt then like she'd been watching us. Missy yanked away the spiral, slammed it shut and popped up. Clanging up those metal stairs to go inside, Missy's legs sounded heavy and her head was down and Ma Ha was just standing there, giving me the stink eye.

Like Missy, Ma Ha had been pretty once too. You could tell. But now Ma Ha's cheeks drooped and her dark eyes rested in little bowls of purple. You got the feeling she was mad at Missy for rocking what she'd lost.

Well, after that, whenever I came around, something caught in Ma Ha's face soon as she saw me. And I just knew she was downing me inside her head. I'd be thinking: *Is you looking at me sideways or is that just your pan face?* Whatever it was, Ma Ha made sure to shoo Missy away to sweep up the back or grumbled for more ice and Ma Ha, or maybe Unc, would finish my order like they were trying to hurt someone before hurrying me out. Sometimes the food wasn't even cooked right.

Two days before everything got crazy, we sat on a low stone wall at the playground. I'd swung past Democratic Best after work. We'd set it up so that, when she could, Missy would follow me down there after I got my order. At the jungle gym, little kids played at monkey bars or sat pretzel-style counting off some clapping game.

"Took you long enough," I said.

She lit a cigarette and took a long pull. "I had to wait for my mom to go next door."

"Why they like that?" I opened my Styrofoam tray of food.

"I don't usually talk to boys around here."

"So?"

"They don't want me to make a mistake."

"Who they want you to talk to?"

She punched out a short, disgusted breath. "A Korean realtor."

My eyes rested on her mouth where her top lip was bell-shaped. Her hair, inky and shiny, was swept up in a bun, stuck through with two orange pencils. Little wisps hung down and every so often she'd brush them back from her cheeks.

Missy hadn't gone to a zone school—Patterson or Lake—like everyone else around there. Her parents had paid for one of those private schools where the girls wore plaid skirts and rode a cheese bus that came right to their house. In the afternoon, her father used to be at the curb, ready to chaperone Missy those twenty feet to the door.

"So I guess they're not giving me no chance?" I asked.

"Probably not." She bumped her shoulder against mine. "You are not Korean or a realtor."

I wheeled my fork in slow turns through the fried rice and then closed the container for later. I don't like to eat mad. Sits on my stomach wrong. "Well," I said, "it's not like I'm one of these hood-lums that's always cussing or feels some need to act out." I plucked up the front of my zebra work shirt. "I keep a job. I even watch the history channel."

Missy wagged a finger, imitating her mother, "*Rose not like fungus. Make a problem.*"

"Yeah, what's she say about keeping you back there in a dirty apron, chopping onion all day?"

She shrugged and passed me a small, white paper bag she'd smuggled out. It was a cookie, pebbled with chocolate chips. I set it with the other food.

"You're too pretty to be in a apron, anyway," I said.

"She doesn't think like that."

Other girls I talked to, I held back compliments 'cause it got their heads too big and then they'd want the world, but Missy, she wasn't like that. "She oughta," I said. "Because, one day, someone's gonna put you on a magazine."

She dropped her eyes and smiled shyly.

"What?" I said. "That's what they do with pretty girls like you." We were quiet, and I sipped my half and half.

"You'd have to know my parents to understand," she said.

"Don't I?" I asked. "I been eating their food half my life."

"That's the store," she said. "Home, *inside*, is different."

The Has were so far up Missy's busi-ness, she had to cook up some wild lies before they'd let her out to the movies with me: that I didn't like girls, tutored kids at the chum bucket, stayed in church Sundays, that I'd be starting college for accounting soon, and that we'd be meeting old friends of hers from school at the theater.

About noon that day, I got on the phone with Missy to hook everything up: fajitas at The Can Can downtown. Then to that new Transformers movie. Popcorn. Sprites. Those little Jujubes I know she likes. Soon as we hung up, I started cleaning—a girl like Missy would expect a sanitary toilet if we came back to my place after. And I was so amped-up that, in between sweeping and scrubbing, I knocked out fat sets of push-ups and crunches.

I can look like a pretty-boy when I want and that night, I made sure I was looking fresh—proper-like too. When I got up to Missy's, I had on a sky-blue, Polo button-down, flat-front, cream khakis looped with a shiny black belt, and gray Pumas right from the box. I also thought that maybe some of the fellas around the way would see us crossing the park and, pretty as Missy was, I liked the idea of that.

Missy had told me to wait out front, she'd be looking out for me. I'd been out there less than a minute when a dude came bopping up the block. When he got close, he stopped, snapped his fingers, and said, "Say, ain't I seen you at Foot Locker?" I couldn't place his face, but I didn't think anything of it, told him yeah.

"Bet," he said, happy for nothing. "I knew I knew you."

I was quiet.

"You working this weekend? 'Cause I'm trying to get that employee discount."

I was like, "Nah, bruh. Can't do it."

"Ain't those new Jordans about to drop?"

"Saturday," I said. "They gonna be tight."

"What—baby blue and silver?"

"Blue and silver or red and black. Take your pick."

"So what's up?"

"Wish I could help you out." I cut a glance up at Missy's windows.

Dude caught a real attitude. "That's petty, man."

"Hey, I'll never make manager giving away the hot flavors."

"Bet you don't tell your peoples that when they come up there."

"My peoples don't come up there," I said. "And if they did, it wouldn't be with their hands out."

He squared himself, close enough now that on his stone face I could smell the sour-medi he'd been smoking. "You a damn lie," he said. "And I didn't ask you all that."

In a minute, Missy would be stepping out looking amazing, probably wearing those skinny jeans and a white halter, and we'd be on our way to those good steak fajitas and this dude wouldn't have no one to jaw at and would've just bounced. But looking in dude's eyes, I could see that this Stone Face wasn't going nowhere. I might look funny, might have a funny name, but I can handle myself anywhere. People used to say I favor Vin Diesel, and I guess I do a little. 'Cept my eyes are like two full moons and my people are all from another side of the world: a father in Brazil and a Canadian mother—one of those white girls that used to lock down her hair in corn rows so tight you knew she was wacky bats. If I grew out my hair, you'd see these countries in me. Plus, I'd rather listen to Wyclef or Santana or even Adele than any of these phony gangstas on 92Q rapping about how they're the realest cat they know. Call me what you want: I'm a green-eyed, red-boned, bull. Showtime if you want it.

"Do I know you, bruh?" I asked. In my head I was trying to

figure out how I can do this and keep my clothes clean, so when I hit him, I was punching a hole in the sky to square this whole thing up front.

But that's not how it went. He was quick and I barely caught him and when he swung there was a corkscrew squeezed into his fist, which he socked through my cheek piston-quick. I knew at once he'd hurt me because I felt that metal on my tongue. Then I was like, if I'm going to Johns Hopkins, he's going to Johns Hopkins.

Fast, it was all happening so fast. But I stayed cool and got in close. We were tussling in the Has' rose bushes and then he was under me and I knew I had him and that he would have to deal with how I dug up in him. Thorns like barbed wire raked hell out of my neck and arms, but I did not feel them till later. When Missy came out and saw me and dude in the roses, both of us messed up, she started screaming, *No! No! No!* , kind of fanning her hands like a bird too hurt to fly. I felt her tugging on my belt, trying to pull me up, and I let her.

I don't remember climbing those steps. But inside the Has' house, I worried dude would be getting up and following us in, so I put my shoulder into that door and turned the lock myself. With my back pressed against the jamb, I stood sucking air. The house smelled like cooked cabbage and Lemon Pledge. I guess I looked bad because when Missy turned and saw me—*really saw me*—she hid her face in her hands.

Down the hall she yanked me. On the bright hardwood floors my face trailed red pennies. A lacquered table with little ivory turtles and a brass dragon swam at me. The Has' home, I realized, was different from other houses nearby, or even their dingy carry-out next door.

She turned me into a bathroom, and I felt my face being guided into running water. The white sink bowl went winey dark. I peeked up and noticed then that she'd gotten her hair done—it was straight and shiny with gold highlights, parted on the side under a butterfly beret—and she was wearing this candy cane mini-skirt and platform sandals and her long legs, olive and smooth, looked so primo I could've died right there. In the mirror she was biting her lower lip to quit from crying. A wave of hurt worse than my mouth ran through me. I dunked my face under the faucet and rinsed out grainy bits of broken tooth. I checked the mirror again and saw a Halloween mask staring back. My good clothes were soaked through, destroyed. Blood pooled under my tongue. I had to work from swallowing it. I spat and sucked more tap and swished it around, and it was then that I realized that I was steady losing sink water straight out my cheek.

This fool had really gone and messed me up.

I swore and spat again. Blinking away some drops, I turned to Missy. "You look amazing," I told her. But it wasn't Missy anymore standing in the doorway. It was Ma Ha, her mouth cranked open like a stuck Pez dispenser. She was locked in on something near my shirt collar. She swallowed a wounded grunt—*Oh!*—that was full of pain and humiliation. Slowly, she reached and picked something off my shoulder. Her face froze as she held it up to the light: a crinkled white rose petal, all oily with blood.

Out of Ma Ha's crumpled face came a shriek more animal than woman. None of it was English, but it was still annoying. I waved her away and tugged the bathroom door closed because I like a little privacy when I'm watching sink-water spout from my cheek like one of those lawn statues you see outside Home Depot.

The next time the door opened, it was the police.

I was eight days in bookings.

People say that when you're first dropped in that bullpen you better find somebody you know and dap 'em up, let these hoods see you cool with somebody. But the blank faces just stared and gave way like they'd never seen someone left back by the meat wagon. A path opened to a corner, and I eased through and slid down in it.

On the second day, before I got my stall, they took me to the little infirmary. The nurse was tired and should've already been home by the time she got to me, and she threaded my stitches like the hurry she was in. I could feel my cheek wrung tight. Much later, even after I'd gotten used to it, my tongue couldn't help circling the whirled-up knot of flesh that nurse left inside. On the third day they took me into a hearing to say I would see the judge in five days.

During those days, I lay on that iron shelf while my eyes traced endless figure eights in the diamonded steel mesh, and I thought about what a fool I was. It wasn't the first time I'd gotten jammed up, but it had been a few years, and I'd told myself I wasn't coming back. I'd tried to do right: took the slow money at Foot Locker, and stopped hanging with the wrong crowd. Left those corners alone, stayed more to myself.

And yet here I was, again.

In court they make everything sound worse than it is. The judge looked like one of those eaters that gets kicked out of Old Country Buffet: a wheezy, can't-help-himself kind of roly-poly—like its work for him just to stay upright. I pictured pasty folds of fat stacked under the black robe and imagined all the dudes' futures he'd sifted in his stubby fingers.

Now he held mine.

He faced me and asked if I had anything to say. It was like a trick, though, because straight away he started sliding papers to a deputy, giving him instructions. And when he turned back to me, he was already talking again. "You're going to be placed in a program called Violins for Freedom." He pushed his glasses back up his glistening nose. All his decisions had already been made. "You'll be studying the violin. An instructor will be assigned to you and there will be lessons that you will have to learn. Meeting the terms of your parole will depend on it."

That afternoon I was out and riding the 13 home.

Everyone on my block—the regular down-the-hill crew: kids mostly that should've been in school—had already heard everything and greeted me like I'd saved the world. They could hardly wait their turn to get at me—the meat of our palms popping and snapping loud enough for the whole block to hear—pouring out a chorus of *you got him, man, we heard you messed yo up, he ain't coming back.*

But I had nothing to celebrate.

I saw that I hadn't missed anything. The corner boys went back to their spots, churning on their little strip: "Page turner—got that page turner." Here came Chief, hunched over his wire cart—elbows better than hands, the way he steered it—not yet embarrassed enough to hide the rotten gray something growing on his big toe, trying to sell off the last of his pack: "Loose ones! Loosies!" The plastic bottles and bags scattered in the bus shelter looked the same as always, like that was where the wind had swept them and where they would stay. Little kids were ducking in and out of their hideaway—a brick-charred vacant, gone hollow straight through and sprouting leafy trees. And from a breeze lifting out of the alley came that dead rat smell to make you think you're it.

I climbed the stairs to my third floor efficiency. Inside it smelled like something stuffy trapped in the shadows. I shimmied open one window and then the other. A breeze skipped along the sill.

It was strange somehow to be back in my place among my things. Take away the bathroom, it was just one room, but it was mine, had been mine since I'd aged-out of my last group home two years before.

Had I been away only eight days? A lot had happened, and I knew the tide of consequences was still rolling in. I stood beside the wobbly card table I usually ate at and pressed a finger on its edge, checking for the familiar see-saw in its legs.

I'd forgotten how much I'd straightened up for Missy: No plates in the sink, no trash in the can. Pots tucked in the oven, pans hooked on the peg board. And from Door Busters on Monument, a new bedspread looking like a hot iron creased its edges. I'd even taken a wire brush to the caked-in grime that had set into the stove-top long before I got there, but some things you can't get clean.

It felt like I should call someone, tell them what happened. But there was no one I really wanted to talk to, except Missy. I've known people—grown men—who couldn't stand to be by themselves, and I knew I was not like them. A lot of my life I'd been alone, and it had been alright. Now the quiet was on me, heavy and lonesome.

Jail stink—some lowlife rotation of lice disinfectant, no account heads sweating through their underwear, stopped-up toilets—was still in my nostrils. I stripped off my crusty shirt and khakis. In the bathroom mirror, my busted-up face stared back. I was remembering how different Missy looked in her going-out clothes, and I began to wonder what she ever saw in me anyway. I'd never thought she'd go for me. Maybe now she wouldn't.

I stayed under the shower until the steam quit and the water went cold. Afterwards, I changed into clean shorts and a v-neck tee and dropped on to the bed.

I plugged in my phone and laid it on my chest, waiting for a charge. I knew better than to just go bopping back into Democratic Best. The Has wouldn't want me anywhere near Missy, or them, again. Not after what I did.

After a while I called work, hoping my shifts hadn't been given away. "We're busy here, Bahia," the manager said. "I got a store to run." He hung up.

The noise in bookings had been constant, and I'd not gotten much rest. I was grateful to be clean and in my own bed again and, lying there, sleep flickered over me.

The next day I had to be to Violins for Freedom at noon. I hadn't given it too much thought, only that whatever it was going to be, I wanted to get it over with. I was up early and rolling.

A letter and map from the court bailiff showed a starred address by the water. The east side I knew all over, and walking didn't bother me because you can kind of think things through while you go along.

I set off, making sure to go well around Democratic Best. It was a blue sky with white clouds tied in knots. I cut a diagonal across the park where over the last few years people had come in and fixed up these row homes—slowly at first, then all at once. And I'd wondered where all the money came from to scrape off the flaky paint and put on fresh, to hang the heavy, paneled-wood doors fitted with the shiny brass hardware, to solder the new copper flashing over the bay windows and tuck the flower boxes under them. And walking those blocks, you could feel lost, like you'd crossed into another world you no longer belonged in.

In the distance the expressway ramps dropped into downtown like undone laces. Homeless would be under them, stretched out on their blankets in the heat. It wasn't far from where my mother had once lived. I'd always had it in my mind that she might be under there, among them. It was stupid to think so. She could be anywhere, or nowhere.

I sloped off and took turns going along the streets that ran in straight shots down to the water—Wolfe, Durham, St. Ann. Another twenty minutes and I was trailing along the expensive shops by the water, past valet parkers posted-up in red coats, and little boutiques where all they sold were perfumes no bigger than a house key.

At last I reached the address. It looked like any of the storefronts around there, a travel agency on one side, some kind of bank running lit-up fractions across the glass on the other, and I felt like I must be in the wrong place.

But when I tugged open the frosted glass door and stepped into the empty hardwood lobby, I saw it. A uniform at a backroom door: a cop? A CO? A deputy? Someone from parole and probation? It was the law, whoever he was. Black stripe down the side of his grey pants and a sidearm on his waist.

Holding out my paper, I stepped forward. He patted me down, and while he ran his crackling wand between my legs, I realized the place must've been a hair salon once. Cushioned swivel chairs were planted before a long row of mirrors, and there were two shampooing sinks with that u-shaped dip where customers once lay their necks. The guard told me to sit tight. Sweat marked my t-shirt, and, sitting in the chair he'd pointed at, the cool air felt nice.

Soon, the door opened and a very old man came out. He knew my name already and said it funny. Instead of Bahia Salazar, he said *Bajia Zalazar*.

His head was a pale dome. Piled-up silver brows arched over grey eyes. The skin on his cheekbones was like netted discs. He wore a crisp dress shirt tucked into dark suit pants.

He showed me into his studio where he told me I was there to learn the violin, that, if I didn't like it, I could choose to be remanded instead, that his name was Boris Wollensky and that he was to be my teacher. His accent was not easy to understand, and I had to play back the sounds in my head to make out the words. The guard, whose face gave away nothing, hung close to the door.

I looked around. It was laid out nice in there: a plush ruby-colored couch and matching ottoman, a tasseled Oriental rug. Against the wall, a rack of violins stowed in open cases. Sheet music was propped on stands. Framed, gray pictures of tuxedoed white dudes playing the violin hung on the wall. None of them had normal names either: *Heifetz. Szigeti. Piatigorsky.*

His studio had a little kitchen with a fridge and a small sink set into a stone counter. He'd been fixing himself tea, and he went back to it. Under his dress shirt, I saw his back was kind of stooped and boxy. From an electric kettle he poured steaming water over a cup that looked like somebody's good china, squeezed lemon over it, and left it to cool.

"Have you heard a violin before?" he asked.

"Yeah, it's what they play when the movie's about to be sad."

"That's it? Nowhere else?"

"Pretty much."

"Booo," he said.

"You asked."

"Maybe you're clogged." He pointed to his head.

"Maybe I never been around 'em."

"Open your ears."

I was watching him. He was very old, but there was something lively and game in the way he carried himself. He handed me a laminated, fold-out diagram of a violin, and told me to open it. Along the neck, notes ran up and down, side to side, or spiral—couldn't tell which. It all looked the same.

He took up a violin and held it parallel to the diagram. "First assignment: find the notes on your violin, memorize them." He ran his finger down the neck. "Low to high"—then back up—"High to low. All four strings."

"How long I gotta do this?" I asked.

"What is the length of your probation?"

"They gave me a year."

His lids lowered and his lips curled down. "God willing."

"I gotta keep coming down here for a year?"

"Twice a week," he said. "Take it or leave it."

An irritated catch snagged in my throat.

"You must practice every day"—he eased the violin into the case, folded it closed, snapped the clasps and handed it to me—"for your freedom."

I left Wollensky's, a violin crooked under my arm, like I could hide it. Along the way, I was popping into stores and filling out applications: Under Armour, Dunkin Donuts, Jiffy Lube, Royal Farms. Each time I came to that felony box, I checked no. Footlocker had skipped the background check. Maybe I'd get lucky again.

I dropped the violin at home and beat it over to the playground Missy and I had been sneaking off to before I got locked up. On the stone wall, I sat, looking at my phone. After a while, I keyed in a text: *I'm here. At our spot. I'll wait for you.*

It felt like forever that I was waiting and after a while I took up a stick and began turning it between the loose stones in the wall, digging out the dusty grit.

My breath skipped when I saw her coming down the steps, reaching back, undoing that white apron. When she got close, she lobbed the balled-up apron at me. I picked it up near my feet and began folding it neatly. She had on a white tube top and yellow capris, a little canister of pepper spray clipped on her hip.

Shame burned my cheeks. "You're not gonna mace me, are you?"

She squinted, her face full of questions.

I hesitated. "How you doing?"

She took my head in her hands, staring at the buttoned wound healing on my cheek, and everything I wanted her to say came into her eyes.

"I'm sorry," I said.

She sat and eased into my arms. Her hair was in my face and her breasts pressed against me. Behind the kitchen grease, she still smelled nice—shampoo, lotion, perfume, never knew what it was because Missy used to mix up her smells.

"I've been worried," she said. Tears hung on her long lashes.

We were quiet.

"I called your job," she said. "They didn't know anything."

"I don't think I work there anymore."

She was watching me.

"How I look?" I asked.

"Like trouble." She laughed.

Softly, I passed my thumb over her cheek, smoothing away a tear.

"I didn't know what happened," she said.

"I ain't altogether sure myself."

"Who was he?"

I shrugged. "Just some out the way yo come around to mess things up for somebody else."

"I thought maybe he was someone you knew."

I rubbed the back of my neck. "First time."

I took her hand in mine. Grey and green paint smudged the tops of her fingers. "How're you doing with your pictures?" I asked.

She did not answer but leaned in and kissed me. It was nice— kind of salty like the Has' food, and soft the way she held my face in her hands. We stayed like that and it felt good just to be with Missy again, kissing on the playground.

After a while, Missy dug in my jeans pockets and pulled out my phone. She checked the time. An hour had gone by like nothing.

"I gotta go," she said, getting up.

I reached for her hand. "Don't," I said. "Please. Stay."

She unwrapped a piece of Bubble Yum and started slowly chewing.

Her hand was still in mine. "If I hit your phone later," I said, "you gonna answer?"

"Maybe."

We were climbing the steps to the sidewalk. I was dying to be alone with her again. "Promise?" I asked.

Then she was popping bubbles, walking backwards, watching me. "You can't promise maybe."

Some people took me for illiterate—talked to me slow, like I can't do for myself, or I never learned listening skills. But I had a good head for numbers—teachers used to tell me—and I was never one of those kids in class who didn't trust his own answers, so learning to follow the music on the treble clef was not hard for me.

Monday and Thursday afternoons, I went to lessons at Wollensky's studio. Each time I clamped my jaw on that chin rest, the violin felt dumb small, like a stupid toy for embarrassing me, but I found out soon enough that old man was nothing to play with. The other felons in Violins for Freedom never lasted. Wollensky rode them down, right to the last.

While I sat waiting in that styling chair for my lessons, I could hear Wollensky putting it to them: the ones that took him for a joke, the ones that got to jawing with him, the ones that tried to duck him out, skip lessons, and then slide on in like everything was cool, the ones that assumed just showing up—*I thought I was maintaining*—was enough.

When Wollensky got mad, his tongue had to work extra to get his words out. He'd be picking dudes apart, his English getting worse and worse, and sitting there, next up in the rotation, I would swivel an ear towards the studio's closed door and listen to the strange sounds he made. He'd switch up his *w*'s for *v*'s, get stuck on his *l*'s, tack a *k* at the end of his *ings*, and drag his *r*'s half back to Russia. And when Wollensky said, "*Ve* are not *rrrr*unning-*k* a charity," he wasn't lying.

For a while, other felons shuffled in and took their place. Wollensky dealt with them just the same. A bunch of them quit from the jump. Couldn't take it, said they'd rather jail than learn a violin. And so they did. With my own eyes, I watched the law roll in, four deep, and snatch dudes up for violating the terms of their probation.

Missy and I kept up our playground dodge, hiding from Ma Ha and Unc and the others. I guess we started to think we were pretty slick because it began to feel like a kind of game, sneaking around, getting itchy that one of the Has might be slinking down those playground steps on us.

Out there, she never let me go past feeling on her ta-tas, but I didn't press it because I was happy for what we had, and I didn't want to spoil the good feeling of being together. If our playground kisses were ever going to go any further, it would be because Missy wanted it as bad as I did.

One day she aimed her phone at me, clicking close-ups, and told me she was working on a portrait.

"A portrait?" I asked. "You mean like a picture?"

She nodded.

"For real? You're putting me in your spiral?"

She looked at her phone, distracted. "Aren't you listening, Bahia?"

I shook my head, smiling. "Your people aren't gonna like that."

"They don't like any of it anyway." Our legs dangled over the wall, her heels tapping stone. "It's not like I'm gonna stop. They can't make me stop. I'd probably explode if I did."

"I wanna see it?"

"It's not ready."

"How much you got to finish?"

"I don't know."

"How can't you? You're the one making it."

"It's not lo mein."

I was happy. Nobody had ever done something like that for me.

I don't know why it felt good just to sit and talk to Missy. Normally, I don't say too much to people, and it was only much later that I realized that there on that left-behind playground the city had let go, I'd gotten carried away and given Missy the whole sad story. Things I hadn't spoken of in years. Told how I was born uptown at Sinai and that my father named me after the town he came from. Told how I used to be scared of my mother's teeth, which were as jagged and grey as a monster's from all the crystal she'd done. Told how my father—before they got him—had been here so long, fixing up houses, that he'd forgotten it wasn't his country. Not a lot had scared my father, but immigration at the door had.

"It was bad in DSS?" Missy asked.

"For them," I said. "I wore those people out." Then I told the names of the placements I'd been through and the ones I AWOLed out of, counting them off on my fingers.

We were quiet.

"You know how kids are," I said. "When you're seven, all you know is you want to be with your father."

She listened, waiting.

"I'm pretty sure he must've got jammed up at the other end," I said. "No way he'd have fostered me out like that if…" I let my voice trail off.

We were quiet and then Missy said, "Well, he could've been Vincent Van Gogh and if they decided he didn't check the right box on one of their forms? It's *ahn yung*. That's not your fault or his."

Inside the monkey bars, a little boy was passing two flattened soda cans between the slatted poles, tilting with them, making engine noises.

"Who's Vincent Van Gogh?" I asked.

"A painter," she said. "Like me."

"He's good?"

"He was amazing."

"What'd he put in his pictures?" I asked.

"Different stuff. Stars. Landscapes. Potatoes."

"Potatoes?"

"Sometimes."

"Why'd he do that?"

"I can't tell you. You have to *see* it."

I was thinking how if you stare at something long enough you can start imagining all kinds of things in it, and I wondered if that's what Missy had done. "They got him in museums?"

"All over the world."

"Oh, if they got him in museums, it's a wrap," I said. "He must be good."

She nodded.

I was twenty years old then and the only person I'd ever loved was my father and I'd not seen him in a very long time. Those words— *I love you*— were not words I'd told any girl, ever, but I was hung up enough on Missy that I was ready.

It's like she knew, too, because she smiled, letting that twinkle stay in her eyes, and clamped my birds baseball cap low on my forehead.

And I was sure it was love because it was still there, inside me, long after she was gone.

By the time Wollensky started me on simple scales, we were bumping heads. I'd be playing my lesson and, while he listened, he'd dip his face into that fridge and stand picking at the food on those shelves: little jars of pickled herring or trays of pink salmon. Then he'd turn back to me and kick at my heels. "Feet together. Violin up. Wrist back. Your pinky —is it mush? *Curl* it."

When Wollensky pinned my thumb lower, and braced my pinky into an arch, the smells of those hors d'oeuvres he'd been sampling would be on his breath: sardines, chicken livers, deviled eggs. All that.

A Monday rolled around when I was ready to snap. It had been about a month by then—long enough that people had gotten used to seeing me carrying around a violin case and stopped asking what it was—and I'd practiced like I was supposed to. An hour one day, a half hour another, a little something that morning. Had little pads on my fingertips going white from it. Even got a cramp in my shoulder. But it hadn't been enough for Wollensky and now old man was leaning on me and I wanted to take that violin and crack him over the head with it. I dropped my eyes and held the instrument at my side, breathing hard.

"Why don't you just walk out?" he asked. "What are you waiting for?" Crumbs and whatnot had gotten behind his lower lip, and his tongue was swishing around in there.

"I'm alright," I said.

"Violin is not for sweet chops."

"*What?*"

"Violin is not for sweet chops."

Even if I didn't always understand his words, I knew when someone was cracking slick, and I didn't like it. "What're you saying?"

"You're not a sabra. I thought you were a sabra."

"I don't know what that is."

"You stink," he said. "That's what."

He took the instrument and settled it under his chin. He did not play a boring scale, but a song he called a Hebrew Melody. In his hands the instrument cried beautifully and you felt like Wollensky was wringing the notes from your own heart. The man had a waxy face, teeth full of metal, silver caterpillar eyebrows, flesh hanging off his neck—what they call it, jowls?—and arms spotted the way old people's get, but when he drew the bow across those strings, he killed it. His notes were butter, his stroke was a feather, and the music that jumped out of that little box when he played it filled the whole room.

"Try it again," he said, handing it back.

I got myself together, set the violin back on my shoulder and then dragged the bow across the strings, squeaking and chirping.

"*Mazel tov.*" He cupped his hands over his ears. "You're not sawing wood. This is violin."

My frustration hissed out in a long pent-up breath. "You want too much." I sat. The violin and bow lay across my lap and I folded my hands over them.

He took a seat and we watched each other, his grey eyes watery and searching. You had to give it to Wollensky: Old as he was, he still kept himself up. I was admiring his pressed, herringbone slacks, the sharp collar on his dress shirt—clothes that fit him like a tailor had cut them that morning. Shoes—Magnanni's, I think—so soft you couldn't hear him shuffling around beside you. And the way he kept his tea cup on that little matching plate, one never far from the other, you couldn't help feeling he must've been somebody once.

"Your parents—where are they?" he asked.

For what seemed like a long time I did not answer. I wanted him to look away, but his eyes never left mine. "My father was deported."

"Where?"

"Why does it matter?"

We were quiet.

"It was a long time ago," I said. "So I can't answer nothing about it."

"Your mother too?"

A way-back image rose in my mind: my father circling a finger by his temple to describe my mother's kind of troubles. "I'm not for sure."

He drew his seat closer. Our knees almost touched. He took up my left hand, turned it over and back. His thumb searched along my knuckles, rippled and dug out with old scars. He straightened my fingers, flattening them between his warm palms, softly pressing the joints.

"What's the problem?" I asked.

"What did you do to your hands?"

"Accidents," I lied. "What you a doctor or something?"

"A doctor would know better."

"They look bad?"

"What do you think?"

"I *zhink* you wouldn't know too much about it, G." I said. "It gets rough out here."

He waited, measuring me with those heavy grey eyes. Then he stood and began tidying pages of sheet music. "Such things as this," he shrugged.

"What?" I asked.

"What *what*?" he answered, mocking me.

"What you doing?"

"Our decisions are our own, Bahia," he said. "That's not a nothing."

I felt he was about to give the guard at the door some signal to bust in and haul me out.

"Even when they are to our cost, they're our own." He stretched out a hand, flicking his fingers. "It has been enough. Give me the violin now."

I looked at him: he was serious. "No, sir."

He reached for the instrument, and I shielded it, turning away. "You can't do that."

"You don't practice, Bahia. You don't really care."

"I do practice."

"What you're doing—this fumbling—it's not practice. Twiddlers I don't need."

"I'm not," I said.

"You're not what?"

"I'm not what you called me."

He wagged his head, his tongue hunting behind his teeth. Then he stepped back and raised his hands from his sides, motioning me up. He clapped and barked out the notes of a short scale: "G, A, C flat,C, D, F, G. Begin."

This I could do. I stood once more and started playing the scale. But each time I finished, he'd holler *again!* If I was flat or sharp, he'd hum in the corrected note, fixing up where I went off. He knew the mistakes I'd make before I even made them. Over and over, he had me run it back.

Again!

Again!

Again!

Again!

It went on like this, the old man pressing in, calling me out, little bits of white spittle bunching at the corners of his mouth. After so many times, I stopped. "I think I got it."

"Your ribs," he said, "take them off your hips."

"I'm ready to play something else."

"What do *you* have to do with any of it?"

"I'm saying."

"Hum it. Show me *your* ready."

I can sing a little bit, but now I hesitated, trying to remember the sound of the notes I'd just played. I mumbled a few sounds, then stopped.

"You see this?" A smug laugh slipped out. "Why should anyone listen to you? You don't even hear yourself."

On the phone that night, Missy must've heard it in my voice. She kept asking about my lesson. Usually, I didn't let on too much. People who got their head on straight—like Missy—can be turned back by fear. They smell trouble and veer away. If Missy knew how close Wollensky was to sending me back, she might realize she deserved better.

"You know how old people get," I said. "He's just hard-headed." I spread a bag of frozen tater tots on a pan, slid it in the oven. "You think it matters if I pre-heat this oven?"

"What are you making?"

"Tater tots."

"Tater tots, no," she said.

"I didn't think so neither."

"I want you to look out for yourself," she said.

Outside a police siren squawked. I went to the window. Across the street, two knockers were pulling up in a Crown Vic where another cop had sat three kids on the curb.

"What I need to worry about that old man for, when I got you to talk to?"

"I'm being serious."

"I'm cool," I said. "I can deal."

"Then why do you sound like that?"

"Sound like what?"

"Mad," she said. "Or like you're about to get mad."

Missy wasn't going to be bluffed out. She already knew me too well. "How you think I look holding a violin?"

She was drinking iced tea, and I could hear cubes rattle against the glass. "Like a violinist."

"Exactly," I said. "I don't know who they think I'm supposed to fool, but I don't like embarrassing myself. Gets old."

"What's this guy expect?" she said. "You're just starting out."

"That's the thing. He doesn't go by that."

"What's he go by?"

"He's not gonna let something slide just 'cause I'm a beginner," I said. "He's particular like that."

We were quiet.

"This is crazy," she said.

"Isn't it? And I done it to myself." Outside the kids on the curb had turned their pockets inside it out and a knocker was toeing around whatever had been in there. "I wish I'd never seen that dude," I said.

"You mean"—

"Neither one, matter of fact. They both tricky. One'll put a hole in your face. The other'll get you locked up behind a violin. Can't trust nobody."

"You can trust me."

Nothing came of the jobs I'd applied for. For a while, I kept at it, stepping up to cash registers empty-handed, asking about openings, filling out forms, following up. But you get tired of putting yourself through all that just to hear another *no*.

Until then, my rent had always been on time. Now, the sugar jar was thirty-three dollars from tapped out. Bone dry. End of the line. And I was scared of what could happen to me. Things could turn very quickly. I'd seen it happen before. One minute someone could be doing fine, with a little job and their own place, maybe saving for a car. Then it could all be gone. It happened like that.

I'd stood out on that corner before, grinding for a dollar in a crew of other hustlers, and I wasn't going back to that trap game. But I wasn't taking a number for a cot at the shelter, either.

Landlords don't wait on their money forever. Mine was a Jamaican who liked to cuff his sleeves high up, by his shoulders. He'd been popping up, a wad of keys jangling at his hip, looking to catch me in a lie about being broke. On this day, he knocked and called me into the hall. "I never took you for no slippery eel," he said.

I apologized again, stalling, promised to have his money soon.

He brushed past me, stepped through my doorway, peering inside to see what I had worth selling. Back in the hall, he let out a breath, cussing softly. He looked me over—flip-flops, shorts, a beater—and bit back annoyance. From his wallet, he pulled a card and scribbled a number. "It's a Dalton there. Tell him, I tell you put you on."

"Put me on what?" My hands went up. "I ain't touching no packs, no pills, no nothing."

His face shied back, offended. "It's laundry, man."

On the outside, Downtown Linens was one in a scatter of old, brick and glass-block warehouses, way east, past Edison Highway, and nowhere near downtown. If there'd been people around there once, they'd moved on lifetimes ago. Grass cracked up the sidewalks, and a wobbled line of headless metal stalks ran where the parking meters had once been.

Dalton was another Jamaican, and he didn't seem surprised I was standing in his loading dock. At the next bay, a pair of gassed Mexican men pitched fat bundles of hospital laundry on dollies.

Dalton wheeled a load inside. The rows of split-pocket washers looked new: shiny locomotives chuffing out something bleachy and sweet. He squatted down and unhooked the snatch. The sling tarp fell open and out of this jumble of hospital gowns and bedding, all kinds of crusty oozes and crumbly wastes tumbled. I must've made a face because he started laughing. He lifted a hand and snapped the blue latex glove on his wrist and howled some more into his forearm.

At another washer, the Mexican men handling the nasty loads looked unfazed.

"You want that mean green, don't you?" The Jamaican wasn't

laughing anymore. Still stooped, he flashed twenties from his pocket.

Until you've been on your own with nothing in your pockets, you can't know how rich a couple twenties could make you feel.

Beside me, the machine heaved to life, shuddering as the washer drum picked up speed. The concrete floor throbbed. High up, birds flitted between the ducts, and behind the glass hatch the laundry spun into a single grey zero.

The first song Wollensky taught me was a Czechoslovakian folk song called "Bohemian Brown Bear." It had this corny little two four beat, like clopping horses. No bass. No rhythm. It sounded like nothing I wanted to play, and I couldn't understand what Wollensky heard in it. But he kept riding me.

"The brown bear bounces on the two." He sounded fed up.

"I told you, I'm trying," I said. "If you'd quit rushing me."

His eyes were sick with pity. "Perhaps this is your rainy day?"

"I'm serious," I said.

"Your tummy, maybe, is dizzy?"

"Why don't you give me something good to play?" I asked.

Disgust broke across his face like I knew it would. "Don't tell me," his lips flapped out.

"Dag, Mr. Wollensky," I said. "You gotta make everything hard."

He laughed, a long laugh that he cut short. "I will tell you something. If I live another hundred years, I will still be a stranger here. When I came here, I was younger than you even. No family. No country. No culture. I didn't know a soul. English I knew how to say bathroom. Do you know the next word I learned?"

"No."

"Library."

Veins burrowed like blue worms in his neck. He ran his fingers along the inside of his shirt collar, trying to calm himself. "So tell me, what is so hard about this?" His hand was snapping the sheet music.

I bowed my head. "Don't violate me, Mr. Wollensky. They'll send me away."

"You'll send yourself away. You have volition."

"I'ma do better," I said.

"This music," he said, "it is in you somewhere. Find it. Otherwise it will be too bad for you."

A day came when Missy and I did not sneak over to the playground. Instead, we were able at last to be alone, together, without worrying about her family creeping around or the little kids at the playground watching us.

When I went downstairs to let her in, she was holding a tall plastic bag with something flat and thin in it. A long tattered edge poked out; it could only have come from her spiral. Upstairs, she took out the portrait.

It was me alright, and it looked so real I knew she must've spent time on it. It showed my Orioles cap turned backwards, my brown face, my green eyes, brows dark and straight as a ruler.

"What?" I found the bed behind me and sat down. Then, looking more, I saw she'd given me an expression I didn't recognize—too open or unsuspicious, like the world's so peachy I hadn't been watching my back all my days.

"Don't you like it?" she asked.

"It's amazing," I said. "It's just—you made me kinda soft, didn't you?"

She was enjoying this and did not answer.

I held it away, then close-in again. "It's me and not me."

"You have a lot of faces." She took the painting and propped it on the table. "It's you when you're with me."

I got a tingly feeling, like she saw inside me better than anyone. "That's crazy."

She came over and stood before me and turned her hips for me to untie the apron strings in back. My breath quivered. Missy had plump breasts and one of those cheerleader butts you used to see at school, and everything kind of evened itself out on her. She let me unfasten the button on her shorts and then slowly lower the zipper.

"If they catch me in here, it's gonna be bad," she said.

"They ain't gonna catch us."

"You would say that." Then, straddling my stomach, she pinned back my wrists, her black hair dangling over me, and slowed us down.

Shadows had seeped into the room and you could hear kids playing hotbox outside when we started putting our clothes back on. I walked her up the hill, feeling good, a little dizzy even. The sky was a ribbon of pink, strung low and fading. Street lights clicked on, fuzzy, and there was a lacy, teasing breeze. The houses crouched down in neat stacks, one block after the next, and most weren't as raggedy as by me. Older folks sat on porches playing cards, sipping cans of beer or just bumping oldies on speakers they'd propped in their windows. As we got closer to the blinking neon of Democratic Best, we hung back.

"It's dusk," she said.

I bent and our foreheads touched, our fingers intertwined. "Is that one of those Catholic school words for it?" I asked.

We were beside a little basement fix-it shop, face to face, eyes open, and the smell of sawdust and machine lube drifted up from the open doorway below.

"It's half and half," she kissed me and pulled away. "Makes you feel kinda different about things, like something new is happening."

I stood there, watching her go. I waited until she climbed the steps to her place and let herself in. I could've skipped home. I even started telling myself that we might work this out with her people; the Has could be brought around. And already, I wished she could be there when I got back. Then, just as fast, I burned with envy for some nightmarish Korean dude in a sleek suit riding a sleek elevator in some downtown high rise that Ma Ha would approve of.

When I couldn't get hold of Missy the next day, I didn't zap out. I figured she couldn't get away. A day after that I still hadn't heard anything, and I knew something was wrong. More than two months had passed since I'd gotten out of bookings and during this time we had not gone a single day without talking.

On the third day I walked over to Democratic Best and stood at the diagonal corner, scoping it out. People came and went, going away with their sacks of beef yakamis or chicken boxes or whatever they were having. There was no sign of Missy anywhere.

I had not been back inside Democratic Best since before I'd

fought. Once it had cleared out, I shuffled in like I didn't know any better.

"What's good, Unc?" I said, stepping up to the counter.

He gave me a big smile and acted surprised. "Oh, Number Five."

I looked at him. After everything that had happened, his *number five* sounded phony and I knew he wasn't feeling so swell to see me. I knew he knew why I was there.

He pointed at his cheek, turned down his mouth and groaned.

"Yeah," I said. "He got me good, didn't he?"

His mouth stayed down, stuck on sad.

"It's alright though," I said, "I heal quick."

He clucked out a couple *tisks tisks* before flashing a big smile. "You wan' number five?"

"Why not?" I chuckled along with him. "Number five."

He turned and called back the order in Korean and his voice did not sound nice.

"So, everything good?" I asked.

"Ya, ya," he said. "Working, working. Always busy."

"Don't I know it," I said. "You're a hard worker, Unc."

We were quiet, and I breathed in the familiar peppery tang of Democratic Best.

"So," I asked, trying to sound casual, "Missy alright?"

"Oh, Missy," he said, acting surprised again. "Missy not here anymore."

"Not here?" I asked, half laughing. "What you mean, not here?"

"She go Providence."

"Providence?" I said. "Providence what?"

"Rhode Island."

I felt my stomach drop. "What?"

"Ya," he said.

"What's down there?"

"Up," he pointed.

"Up then."

He began cutting slices of green melon and he ate the fruit right down to the rinds, one after the next. "Better area," he said. "Less problem. Family there too. Butchers." He said this like I was supposed to be happy.

"Butchers?" My throat had gone tight.

"Ya, butchers." His hands scissored the air like he was chopping meat.

I was silent, a little shook. I was thinking, now what the hell's Missy gonna do in a butcher shop?

"When she coming back?" I asked.

He turned up his palms and his shoulders hopped a little. For a long while, I didn't say anything, afraid to ask more. I wasn't sure what to do. If I'd thought it do any good, I'd have yanked Unc over the counter and yoked him up.

They finished cooking my order, and he went about bagging it, putting in plastic utensils, napkins, creasing and stapling the bag shut, and then sliding it before me.

I laid a ten on the counter and he rang it up on the register and brought back my change. I slipped the two singles and the coins in my pocket. "You like Missy's pictures, Unc?" I asked. "You know, the way she draws them?"

He got a sour look on his face like that wasn't important to him.

"You draw pictures too?" I asked.

"No."

"So I guess she didn't get all that talent from you, did she?"

He was quiet.

"What you all—you sent her away? You gonna teach her some kind of lesson?"

"It's family"—

"You said that."

Something wary and fierce flashed in his eyes, and he didn't say anymore.

I slid the bag of food back to him. "You all think you know me, but you don't."

I turned away slowly. In the doorway, I stopped and called over my shoulder, "It ain't bye if you don't say it."

I walked to the end of the block, whipped a tight half-circle and stood, staring back at Democratic Best. My head was not right—not by a long way. Providence didn't have any teams I could think of and I was having trouble placing where it was. I found Rhode Island on my phone. It looked far away—twice as far as New York, and though I'd never been there, I knew that wasn't close. I thought of catching a bus up there—one of those Greyhounds— but where would I look for her and who would I ask for help, and if I did find her, what exactly could I offer?

At home, I sat on the edge of the bed and squeezed my knees into a tuck, kind of rocking with it, before covering my ears so I would not hear the tears I felt coming.

That night and the next day, my calls to Missy went straight to voice mail and my texts were not answered. Soon, her cell service was cut off and, after that, there wasn't even a number to call anymore.

Then it was the next day and the day after. A couple times I tried to worm a different number or her address out of one of the Has, but Unc was finished pretending to be friendly. He just acted busy. Some of the others gave me short smiles or decided they'd forgotten who I was. Twice I saw Ma Ha and before I could even apologize for messing up her house, she showed off like she couldn't stand to look at me, like whatever she hated in me was deeper than any sorry I might offer and nothing she'd be letting go of anytime soon.

Inside my place, I lay back in bed, propped up on pillows, my hands folded under my head. My mind jumped around, turning over everything that had happened. I saw myself the night I fought outside the Has—Stone Face feinting low, hurting me. Mixed in were images of Missy crying that night and Missy acting silly at the playground and how she tasted laying here with me in this bed only a few nights ago. I pulled handfuls of sheet to my face, searching for her scent.

You can think hard about a thing and not get anywhere with it. The portrait she'd made stared from the table. Missy had been right. It was me when I was with her, but now I was alone. And I felt then like this was how things were going to be now, that it was going to be hard on me, and that it had been coming all along, closing in. I just hadn't seen it.

Four in the morning and outside someone was laying on a horn. I'd been in bed, asleep. Now I stood at the window and looked down the block. Wind stirred up the world. In the gusts, yellow light danced on ropey power lines. A billboard ad, white and hanging by threads, ballooned, hung there, then fluttered back. On the corner, the neighborhood crew was on their little strip, turned up. I could see their spotters on opposite corners—kids so green they probably didn't know yet they could get locked up on conspiracy just being near it. Tubed gutters dropped down from rooftops, ran underneath the sidewalks and opened at the curb. In one of these piped-out chutes, they hid their stash. A lanky boy kept going back, dipping low, reaching in there. For a while I watched him: chute, corner; chute, corner; chute, corner. Money changing hands.

In the kitchen, I flicked on the bulb and cut on the gas jet and rinsed a pan. I cracked five eggs on to the hot griddle and let the whites sputter and pop till the edges got crispy. I slid them all on a plate and set it on the bed to cool.

On the edge of the bed, I sat thinking. A cold draft to let you know fall was here slithered through the window frame, and I pressed a pillow into it.

I ate the eggs with wheat crackers. Afterwards, I switched off the light and lay back down. I listened to the voices outside—people bullshitting at the top of their lungs about nothing—and thought about Missy.

It wasn't over. It didn't feel like it could be. And yet, if Unc wasn't lying to me, Missy was in Providence and I was here.

Outside the horn sounded again, frantic.

I'd come up around there, but I was ready for a change. Some place where people took the party inside at night, where I didn't have to wonder whether the mail that came up missing from the jimmied letter boxes in the vestibule was important, or if the lady downstairs running her bootleg electric was about to burn this joint down while I slept.

But there was nowhere I knew to go. And no way to get there, wherever it was. And if my address changed now, how would Missy find me?

The blinds cut up the floor in striped light. I lifted the violin case on to the bed. In that little bit of light, I unclasped the case and passed my fingers over the soft lining. I brought out the violin and lay back down, resting it on my stomach. I drummed my fingers lightly on its body. I felt the tuning pegs, where the strings were wound in tight spools that locked down their pitch, if you treated it right. I plucked the *e*, then the *g*, letting each ping and fade out, before bringing the other back in. After a while, other sounds came to mind: different, little overlaps that might fit.

A violin was a funny thing. Thinning at the waist like a girl, it hardly weighed anything. Yet, it was somehow bigger than it looked. The lightest graze of the bow, and the strings spoke up. And it had a funny smell—all that delicate lacquered wood kept safe from the world in a satin red case.

The melody in "Bohemian Brown Bear" had begun to make a picture in my head. And in the darkness, my fingers found the unseen notes again.

Wollensky said I had a clock in my head to keep time. He gave me a metronome. And you know it's just a tick. Set it how you want. Slow or fast. Wollensky said slow, very slow, and now alone with Missy gone and the cold coming on, that's what I did, kept it real slow. And in the *tick, tick, tick, tick* I saw all the mistakes I'd made: fighting at the Dox or some other club when I should've been happy just shaking off, taking my problems out on people who had nothing to do with them, quitting in the eleventh when I could've finished because a lot of what I learned I still remember—like how people took Copernicus for a joke for showing the circle we make around the sun, or how copper and tin make bronze, or that book about Odysseus, who went through so much just to get home.

But you can't erase nothing. You just carry it along.

Some tenants complained I was too loud, or that it went on for too long. All the ruckus around there, but my violin was a problem.

In the basement, you had to duck your head, bring a flashlight and watch yourself. Beyond a padlocked boiler room, a junk heap spilled off a back wall. I dug in and got between a severed radiator and a shoeshine stand's brass footrests, tipped over a stack of old board games tied up in twine and slid by a headboard. Dust rose and gagged me. I caught hold of a roll of inside-outside carpet, different couch cushions—enough that it took several trips.

Using a box cutter, I layered grey patches of rug across my bathroom floor. I ripped the spongy, yellow foam from the cushions and nailed these squares to the bathroom walls, going high around the shower. Anyone who saw the humped-up floor and puckered walls would've thought something went wrong here.

On the violin there's different ways to hit a note, and you have to hunt for the good ones. A crooked bow, notes fingered even a dime's width off—these'll make a sound that'll hurt you inside somewhere, make you sorry for ever thinking you could do what the old man was asking.

I thought after a while I would hear from Missy: she would buy a burner or put a letter in the mail to me. Maybe she would come back to visit her people and slip away like she used to. Something.

Still, I felt that when Missy was able, she would get to me. And holed-up in front of the medicine cabinet, I worked my pump handle through my intervals—2nds, 3rds, 5ths, flat 7ths, major 7ths—ascending and descending, feeling that pull towards resolution, circling back to catch in the mirror my bow's squealing slips, the scars from those rose thorns now a darker rust against my neck.

The weather turned. Now when I got near Wollensky's I could taste winter, raw and cold, coming off the water along the harbor. Once inside, I would have to beat my hands against my leg, or warm them over his radiator until the feeling came back.

Back and forth, twice a week. It was a lot of walking and along the way, I pictured my scales, testing myself, visualizing the patterns in as many different positions as I could hold in my mind, and singing the notes, just like he'd shown me.

When Wollensky gave me bookwork, I wrote out the exercises on the long study tables at the Enoch Pratt. It was all getting in my head by then and sitting on those library stools, I sometimes heard the fingerings I penciled beside the staff. Or batching laundry at Downtown Linens, a little stray phrase I'd practiced earlier—some choppy chromatic turn or a relay of triads—would come floating in over the pounding drone of those washer drums, and I would feel I was getting closer to having something to show for the work I'd put in. And every so often, my stroke would be so nice—so clean and even and just right—that the sounds coming off that bow seemed to come from somebody else.

My shifts at Downtown Linens didn't start until eleven at night. It was stupid to save a few dollars walking only to risk getting caught along the way by a stick-up boy or some young'un trying to build up his rep. Better to just pay the bus fare. I'd get a good jump on the 22 and start sorting and batching laundry ten, fifteen minutes early. I wondered sometimes what went on in a hospital that people's bedding could get like that, but it never slowed me down. Nobody was ever going to say I didn't work as hard as any Mexican on our runt crew.

And in this way the days blurred and the holidays passed without a word from Missy.

Wollensky upped my lessons. They went from an hour to two, sometimes more. Each time I got the hang of one thing, a harder piece followed. He sent me off with CDs. Back home, I listened to Ernest Bloch's "Baal Shem," Henryk Wieniawski's "op. 15 Variations," Stravinsky and Heifetz. I had not known that I would like this music. The songs were sad—sad and beautiful. That they could be both kind of threw me. Each time I listened, I caught something different, sometimes long after it was over.

It was after New Year's, towards the end of a long afternoon, that Wollensky's face finally gave up the shadow of a thin smile. I was rolling through a static etude I'd studied all week, tip-toeing through the prelude, concentrating, hitting that trill. Wollensky hummed and counted, anticipating the notes before I got to them, scolding and pumping his hands all at once. When I stopped and lifted my face from the sheet music, there it was: an amused satisfaction on the old man's face. His eyes took me in, glistening with something like pride.

"The notes," he said, "are they bringing out feelings?" Hope lifted those furry eyebrows, and I felt naked.

"Yes," I said. "I feel something."

One day I got to my lesson, and the guard who was always posted up in Wollensky's lobby was gone. It was just me and Wollensky. He let me in and asked me to sit. I blew into my cupped hands or tucked my fingers under my arms to warm them. It was strange to be alone with the old man. I felt he'd entrusted me with a duty I wanted to do right by.

"I want you to hear something," he said. He was more keyed-up than usual. He pulled out several pages of sheet music and stood them on the stand. Then he dropped a CD on the stereo. It was an old song by Maurice Ravel called "Pavane for a Dead Princess." We listened. The music seemed to move him. I had to admit, the pavane was very beautiful—pretty and lonely all at once like that kind of music can be. While it played, we kind of forgot ourselves. Wollensky even shut his eyes for a bit because sometimes you can listen better that way.

It was at the cadenza—something about the way he began calling out the notes—that it hit me: he was going to ask me to learn it. I felt my knees getting bouncy.

"I can't play this," I said.

He tipped his eyes toward the speakers. "Listen."

"It's a real nice song, Mr. Wollensky. It really is, but"—

He raised a hand to hush me. "Don't swindle yourself."

I slouched back. He wasn't going to let this go.

He paused the CD. "Why do you practice?"

"I got no choice."

He looked towards the foyer where the guard would normally have stood. His eyes, sad and heavy, hung over the empty space in the doorway.

I was quiet.

He started the music again and over the sound of the violin, he continued to make his points—outlining the song's AABA structure, imitating the slurring legato—scribbling notes on the sheet music.

Using the pencil eraser, he tapped eighth notes along the measures to match the tempo. "Follow the notes," he said calmly. "Where they take you, it's for you only to say."

When he stopped writing, I said, "Why do you spend so much time on me, Mr. Wollensky?"

"What, I should go to Florida?"

I shrugged. "Supposed to be nice down there, right?"

"It's where old people go to talk about prunes. My bowels function adequately. I have no reason."

"Oh," I said. "I never been."

We were quiet.

"Well, you taught me a lot already," I said.

He stood and crossed the room to a small side table. From a drawer he removed a slim box. He brought it over and handed it to me.

I lifted the top and peeled back the tissue paper. It was a pair of black leather gloves, lined with cashmere. They were shiny and thick and had that new-leather smell.

"For your fingers," he said.

After work one morning I rode the bus straight from Downtown Linens to the Enoch Pratt. I wanted to be there when the doors opened, so I could get a computer, and I hung around outside, waiting in the morning chill.

Any pavane is going to have a lot going on in it, and once inside I pulled up videos of different violinists playing Ravel's. They were from all over the world. Istanbul. Tokyo. Other places I can't remember. Old men in tuxedos. Young girls. Each of them sounded a little different and, though they were all good, each had their own way with it. Sitting there, headphones clapped over my ears, hunched into the screen, listening, I must've looked out of place because I noticed that people were sneaking glances at me.

The videos probably didn't look like much to the people watching me—just a bow swishing back and forth. But they would be wrong because even after all the work I'd put in, the pieces of the pavane had not come together yet. The other thing they couldn't know was how badly I wished to shed my mistakes.

Back at my place, I stayed with it, taking it slow, beginning again and talking my way through it, keying my attack to the videos I'd watched or the recordings Wollensky gave me. It was good to hold on to these sounds, to keep them close for when you needed something to carry you through this twisted world.

And while I smoothed out the legato of those long, floating bow strokes, the days grew warmer.

Spring came early.

"Pavane For A Dead Princess" was Ravel's song, but as I worked it out and got closer, I thought less about mechanics or rules and just played, and I felt the music was becoming mine too.

One morning I was at my front window, warming up, loosening the joints on my left hand before starting in with the bow.

Then, through the window, I saw Ma Ha outside. She was walking on the sidewalk across the street. It had been a long time and to see her again, even from up there, twitched my ears. She'd been to the farmer's market across the park. Her arms were heavy with plastic bags. Carrots and greens bulged in them. They pulled at her sides, swaying her hair as she walked. I pressed my face sideways to the cool pane of glass and strained to keep her in sight. A flock of pigeons rose and scattered as she went through. I watched her heading away and then—I don't know what I was thinking, still holding my violin—I started after her. I was down the stairwell and sideways out the front door fast.

On the sidewalk I saw her crossing the next block. I didn't want to run up on her so by the time I got up to the Has', she was already climbing her steps. I must've frightened her anyway because she hurried in and shut the door quickly. I heard a dead bolt catch, and the chain latch.

I stood outside, near the rose bushes I'd fought in the year before. Little green buds were bursting through. Like I said, I'd kind of eased down there, so there was no reason to be gulping air. The windows of the Has' row house looked dark and empty. A few doors down, breakfast smells were coming out of Democratic Best.

People were outside. A woman was shaking out her door mat across the street. Two little girls sat on steps nearby, passing an empty candy box back and forth, trying to make it whistle. An old man was grubbing for cigarette butts by the curb.

When I tucked the violin under my chin and turned back to the Has' house, I could feel the people nearby looking at me, and I knew they'd stopped what they were doing and were waiting for me to begin. And just like Wollensky showed me, I stretched those opening notes of the pavane into the melody, sprinkling in the arpeggios, holding my own, and waiting for the curtains to part.

Dusk and they sat on a lip of sill outside the store, eating tortilla chips, a pair of earbuds splitting Flo Rida between them. Amber was caramel, wore a tie-front blouse and combed up her hair in a platinum faux hawk. Vanka was pale—pale blond—her face a series of starved planes, though she ate everything. Both wore calf-high moccasins and look-alike fringy cut-offs.

"These so dry you can't even call it stealing," Amber said.

Vanka's mouth curled down, still chewing, before she spat orange mush. She read from the bag. "It says, *Dip them in your favorite salsa.*"

"We don't have no salsa," Amber said.

"I shoulda took that too." Vanka twisted the bag between and behind the iron bars where it stuck. A little cloud of gnats floated in, and she clapped at them. "This getting old."

"Give it a minute." Amber stood, the earbud popping free. "Some dummy's gonna ride in here thinking he about to get some. Watch."

Amber crossed the lot to a strand of dirt beside the street. The store, and its cramped parking lot, sat at the top of the Split: a long diamond island that shunted the street to either side. Below the store was a scrap yard where people humped in copper pipes and aluminum siding and window air conditioners and sold them, no questions asked; past that lay Ready Uzed Tires, a 24-hour coin laundry with a sagging, mossy carport, and finally, where the diamond tapered in at the bottom of the Split, was Holiday Motors, an asphalt car lot once, now in puzzle pieces.

She stepped off the curb and looked up the hill. It was quiet. Traffic lights blinked through their cycles. A few cars drifted past. One man tapped his horn, but that was all. She stooped and tore a *Work From Home* sign off its wire pickets and, fanning her face, started back to Vanka.

"I ain't staying out all night," Vanka said.

"Whatever," Amber said. "Talk to me when you're shaking your tail at the Dox."

"For real this time," Vanka said. "I don't want my mom making herself sick waiting up on me."

"You come in the house late enough she'll fall asleep."

"I ain't doing that."

Amber lifted her chin and fanned her neck. "What they call it—heartburn?"

"Reflux."

"You knew what I meant," Amber said. "Anyway, all these dummies out here, it's not gonna take all night to steal their whip."

The air was heavy and still. Sweat glistened on their faces. Street lights, like insect eyes, were popping on, fizzing.

"Oh, snap." Vanka popped up. "I gotta feed the cats."

Amber watched Vanka slip her phone in her back pocket and start for the doors, ear buds bouncing at her ankles.

Along the short aisles, the shelved goods had no obvious organization. Vanka tried to divine a hidden logic in stacking flip-flops behind loaves of white bread, Oodles of Noodles beside cough syrup and headache pills, Ajax powder near a pitted, drop-well freezer of popsicles. At the counter, the Korean owner read a Korean newspaper, smoking a Newport. Vanka set down two cans of tuna and wriggled two singles out of her pocket. He glanced up. Lazy spirals of smoke lifted beside his squinting eyes. He found a can opener from a hook near his knee and cranked off the tops without being asked.

It was a Ford F-250. Amber saw it coasting in from half a block away, dark blue and riding high on enormous tires. She had been texting her sister. She finished and pressed send: *get ur oun bone ass dress an find ur own food.*

Now she was irritated. Her sister was a hoover. She ate the good food Amber put in the freezer and left everybody else the soggy graham crackers in the cupboard. Amber looked up as the truck pulled in, crunching gravel. A man was driving. He had a streaky gray ponytail and a tanned, stubbly face. His heavy forehead pressed down the eyes. For an instant they watched each other. What the man saw was a slinky, high-legged thing in white shorts no longer than her back pockets.

Before Amber turned to face him, she keyed in another text: *an u bettr dont eat my hot pockets.*

She heard the gears shift into park and the engine settle into a low-thrum putter. She looked up.

He kept one wrist on the wheel, and an elbow out the window. She saw the ragged edges of his plaid shirt where the sleeves had been cut off. Below the elbow, his arm was lean and cabled in muscle. "Where's the party?" he asked.

"We're looking for it, Mister."

He put an unlit cigarette to his lips. "Who told you my name?" A rasp was in his throat.

"Just lucky, I guess."

He spat a fleck of tobacco. "That bastard never could shut his mouth."

Amber couldn't tell if he was trying to be funny or just off, but it didn't change much of anything, either way. She smiled. This was easy for her. Boys and men had been following behind her for as long as it had mattered. And she had learned to conserve this power before boys got what they wanted and hit the door.

She stepped closer still. The truck had a shiny, chrome running board and sacks of topsoil weighed down the truck bed. She backed up, admiring the huge machine. "Dag," she said. "What this some kind of monster truck?"

"You like it?" he asked.

"Yeah, it look like it drive nice."

"I'll get you one just like it."

She cut her eyes and glared at him sideways, puckering her mouth scornfully. "Yeah, okay," she said. "I guess you'll say anything."

Across the lot, beside the dumpster, Vanka held the tins of tuna aloft. Cats swarmed her feet. She put their food down.

The man turned to look at the crouching girl with the peroxide-blond hair. "What's your friend doing?" he asked hoarsely.

"Feeding cats."

They watched Vanka petting a calico as it ate.

"Where's your old man?" he said like he knew him.

"You'll probably see my father before me, so you can ask him yourself."

He caught the morbid wit right away. "You don't know that."

"You don't either," she said, close enough now that she began checking her lip gloss in the truck's side mirror. She could feel the warmth from the hood. "And my mom told me to find a nice man to ride us around," she said, still with her face in the mirror.

He offered a grudging, uneven grin. "You're a bad liar," he said, sounding almost protective.

She pocketed the lip gloss. "Gimme a second." Amber turned and yelled, "Vanka!" But the call was ignored.

She started across the lot, switching her hips as she went, certain he was watching. Vanka was still kneeling by the cats. "Can you hurry up?" Amber said, leaning over her.

Vanka did not look up. "He old as shit."

"He ain't that old."

"Like fifty."

"So?" Amber said. "You see what he's pushing?"

A tabby rubbed its chin on Vanka's thigh, and she stroked the animal's neck. She stood and brushed off her knees.

They were walking, together, to the man still in his truck. When they got close, Amber wheeled and hung on Vanka's arm, drawing her in. "Do he stink?" she whispered. "I think he stink."

"It's all that dirt," Vanka said.

Amber glanced at the sacks of topsoil nested in the truck bed, crinkled her nose. "Why dirt gotta smell like ass?"

The cab of the truck was roomy and smelled more of tobacco and new leather than anything else. Mud caked the man's boots and the cuffs of his work jeans, and an earthen powdery gray had dried on the joints of his long fingers. Amber had scooted into the middle and allowed her hips to brush lightly against his. His eyes fell on the smooth expanse of bare leg beside him and lifted again.

"So I guess we can call you Mister?" Amber asked.

"It's alright," he said.

They didn't bother with fake names. They were fifteen and, though it had never come to that, what would the law do with two fifteen-year-old girls but ride them home.

Her eyes scanned the dashboard, checking it out. "What year is this?"

"This year," the man said. "Just made."

Through the open windows the wind felt nice, a wash of briny willow like the roads might be wet though they weren't. Vanka leaned out the window and lifted her face into the rushing air. Her hair flew everywhere. It felt good to be on the way someplace, wherever it would be.

The radio was tuned to a '70s rock station, and Stevie Nicks was singing, *Thunder only happens when it's raining.*

Disgust crushed Amber's face. "Ooh, what is that?"

"That," the man said, "is what we call music."

The girls looked at each other and giggled conspiratorially.

"It sound dead," Amber said, now sounding like she was trying to help the man. "Don't nobody listen to that anymore."

"Not everything has to sound like the zoo got loose," he said.

"Can I change it?"

"Depends what you like."

"Everybody bumps 92 Q." Amber spun the tuner dial.

92 Q was playing Wocka Flocka Flame's "Grove St. Party."

At once, both girls raised their elbows and began shimmying in easy unison to the thumping bass and the lyrics they knew cold.

Their fruity lotion eddied in the whirling air, and he felt a quickening breath—a kind of helpless pant—chase after it.

He took them to an old bar near where he'd lived as a boy. It was one of the last left on a waterfront that had been mostly razed and remade into inlets of high-rise condos and expensive shops and restaurants.

On the broken flagstones going in, he looked off to the tall buildings that in his mind did not belong. "I come up over there," he told them. "Good luck trying to find it."

Inside, they walked past an empty hostess station and slid on to padded vinyl stools at the bar. The hazy tang of dried beer mingled with fryolator burn-off. A few other people sat at the bar or in booths along the wall where metal grates were scrolled up to the ceiling, and the room opened to a planked deck with umbrella-covered tables. It was cooler by the water with a good breeze, and they could hear the canvas umbrellas flapping and the bay slapping lazily under the wooden piers. A row of arcade games was set against a side wall, and in the backroom some men stood around a pool table.

The man was buying. The girls got Long Island iced teas, and he ordered a Miller draft. It was June and the NBA Finals played on a flat screen above the tiered bottles of liquor. Their drinks came in faded glasses, and they watched the game and drank.

After a while, Amber took out her phone. For the third time that day she pulled up a video of a silver-bearded, tribal elder in Uzbekistan stretching his privates half down his leg, then coiling it back up like a cinnamon roll. Something about the solemn deference with which the old man in the video conducted this ritual undid the girls each time.

It was still loading when Vanka pressed in closer. "Here he go."

The girls were hunched over the video, hooting.

The man caught a glimpse and looked away.

Amber pounded the bar. "*Every time* he do that." Then, still giggling, she planted a palm on Vanka's thigh and, leaning across her friend's lap, pushed the screen at the man. "You wanna see it?"

His face was set hard and he leveled his eyes on the girl, never looking at the screen. "Why would I?"

Amber did not like it. She did not like the way he looked at her, but she beamed through it, keeping up the giggle. "What you jealous?"

He tapped out a cigarette from his pack and stood, still watching her. He turned and crossed the bar and put his face sideways to the front window, checking the load of topsoil in his truck. Then he headed out to the deck to smoke. As he passed, Amber spoke into her drink, "Don't nobody want your dirt."

Vanka pressed a shoulder into her. "Chill, Yo."

"He must really think he sure enough somebody." Amber set her elbows on the bar. "This fool is most definitely losing a truck tonight."

Out on the deck a few shore birds hopped away and the man struck a match and cupped it over his cigarette and wondered if the night was shot. Headstrong broads like this one could be more trouble than they were worth: even if you got your party, you might still end up wishing you'd gone to the strip club instead. In his heavy boots and crusted work jeans, he stood before the railing, looking over the harbor, smoking.

At the bottom of the high-rises, new shops along a new promenade glittered beside antique-looking street lamps. A line of glassy moonlight creased the water and, mixed with the briny air, called together images of the old neighborhood that was gone: houses crouched in neat stacks, climbing away from the derrick cranes and eaten-through piers; a line of shivering worshipers outside St. Vincent's, waiting on the hot dumplings, and the seamstresses in the shop window, hunched over Singers, a needle-blur beside fingers.

He toed out his cigarette and stepped back inside. He saw that the girls had put away the phone and were ordering themselves fresh drinks on his tab.

If the evening was going to be saved, he would have to do his part, he figured. He sat again and caught the bartender's eye. When he turned to them, he made an effort to clear his face of judgment. "The place I come up," he said, "it's like it wasn't ever there."

"Where it'd go?" Vanka asked.

"I wish I knew," he said. "Might as well be Q-beck out there."

But Amber had not cooled off, and now the note of wistfulness in the man's voice sounded soft to her. "What you miss it or something?"

He looked at her and understood the girl was baiting him somehow. He did not answer.

"Seems like you feel some type of way about it," she said.

He was quiet.

Amber tipped her head to the Hanover Street Bridge in the distance. "My dad used to wash his clothes in that water."

He waited.

"Rub-a-dub-dub. Sad, isn't it?" she asked. But she didn't sound sad. Instead, pity and hate had curdled into a dismissive, forced cheer. Her eyes followed the birds on the deck. "I'd have done better with one of them pigeons."

He felt the girl somehow transferring responsibility for this neglect on to him, and he wanted to tell her to stick it.

She stood and pocketed her phone, snapped up her drink, and started toward the bank of arcade games.

The bar felt suddenly quiet, though the basketball game still played and the patchy talk of others came and went. A sigh fluttered out of Vanka. She skimmed her glass in circles over the bar's beaded water.

"Egrets," the man said.

"What?" Vanka asked.

"Egrets," he said again. "Those ain't pigeons."

Vanka looked at the birds, hopping here or there. "She probably knows what they are. She's real smart."

"I don't doubt it," he said.

"Probably more mad at herself than anything."

Amber had lowered herself into the cockpit of a race car. The man watched her ripping the wheel one way, then the other, throwing the gear shift up and back, her meaty thighs rocking the pedals, engine noises exploding from the game's speakers.

"She might want to watch it," he said. "She could spoil her good looks behind that bull."

Vanka tried to think of something to say. "It don't last long."

The man acted like he had not heard her. Then he raised a finger and the bartender came and took his glass and filled it again under the tap.

He lifted his face to the flat screen. After a minute he said, "I'm not a Lebron guy."

"I like Russell Westbrook," Vanka said. "He's cute."

OKC was down ten and had just turned the ball over again.

The man took a big swallow of beer. "Cute don't win games."

Although her glass was still half full, the man ordered her another iced tea. Her cheeks were starting to feel hot and puffy, the liquor heavy behind her eyes.

She checked her phone. She didn't have making it home before her Mom. She could see her coming in from work, finding the house empty, angry first, then angry and worried, then just worried, eating Mylantas, feet tucked under her on the couch, listening for the toggled key in the lock, thinking she heard something, muting the QVC channel. Her Mom didn't deserve that, Vanka thought. Then just as fast: her Mom's a worrier. Nothing to be done for it.

She gulped her drink.

"I got some weed at the house. You like to smoke?" the man asked.

For a moment his voice had sounded far away.

"A little sometimes," Vanka answered. "But only if I'm drinking." At once she wished she hadn't said that, but it was too late. He clinked the rim of his glass against hers. She arched her back, drawing away her shoulders, then turned to check for Amber.

The arcade games were empty. She sucked her teeth. "Dummy."

They'd been friends forever: fifth grade, talent show try-outs. That spring they'd learned all the steps to "Putting on the Ritz." After school, at one or the other's house, they'd locked it down: *heel, toe, heel, toe, touch out, touch in, sailor's shuffle.*

They were older now, and still always together, going to the salon for junk nails—rhinestones, hearts, and glitter—skating at Shake & Bake, dancing at house parties or sometimes clubs when they could get in, and still eating their rice with ketchup and butter. "We all we got," they'd tell each other, hooking pinkies, or, "You my main main."

Vanka took out her phone and thumbed in a text: *Where r u?*

In a moment, Amber's reply splashed a luminous blue across Vanka's white tank top: *pool room. Tell yo wash hiz grimy hands.*

Vanka put the phone away and sipped her drink. The liquors raked her throat, and her mind drifted to morning. Waking up drunk, nerves jangly, listening to the house sleep. Digging through the tangle of musty laundry that sealed in the funky smells of other nights like this one, turning sleeves and pants legs right side out. Breakfast would be buttered toast and a thermos of faucet water, and she'd have them on the 22. Walking the hill to ShopRite, pushing aside the break room's heavy plastic flaps, punching in and tying back her green apron. Then all day helping customers carry their bags or collecting carts in the hot parking lot, towing the strapped-up, rumbling line of them out of the corrall, the roar of all those caster wheels rattling parts of her she didn't even know she had, trying to steer around whatever nastiness the parking lot had picked up over night—condoms or diapers, chicken bones or empties, somebody's busted out window, a puddle of throw-up maybe— barely able to hold back that train once it got going.

"You ever swum in the bay high?"

The man was talking again, Vanka realized. She looked into his face, seeing it more clearly now. His skin, underneath the stubble, was spongy.

She shook her head.

The man looked at her bare, slender shoulders. Everything—the little muscles on her arms, the delicate hollow in her underarms, the spaghetti straps on the tank top—seemed inadequate to the cone-swell of breasts inside the push-up bra. She had a pretty mouth. Her lips were full and sinuous. She was, almost despite herself, sexy. Probably wasn't even anything she could do about it.

"It's the best buzz you'll ever have. You get it on your whole body." He was feeling good again and shedding caution.

"I don't know how to swim," she said.

"You can tread water, can't you?"

She shook her head.

He laughed then, showing off his gapped teeth. "Then we'll just lay you on the beach. Let the foam run all over you."

In the ladies' room, they peered into the mirrors above the sinks. Amber touched up her lip gloss and fixed her hair. "What'd I tell you? Once you get in their heads"—she tapped a finger on her forehead—"you see what they're about."

Vanka turned, propped a shoulder against the wall.

"What you drunk?" Amber said.

"Not *drunk* drunk." Vanka made a visor with her hands. "Why's it so bright in here?"

"How many of those iced teas you have?"

"Five, I think. Wait. Yeah. Five."

"No wonder you so soupy."

"I'm not." The bright tiles pressed in and Vanka squeezed closed her eyes again. She rested her hands on her knees.

"You alright?"

Vanka straightened, nodded, opened her eyes.

Amber raised a fist. "How many fingers I'm holding up?"

"You stupid." Vanka giggled, pushing Amber's hand down. "What about Mister?"

"What about him?"

"I don't know," Vanka said. "He doesn't look like someone you wanna see mad."

"Why you say that?"

"Something about him," Vanka said. "I can see him getting real trippy."

"Tough toenails," Amber said. "Let him trip. He can catch the bus too, just like we do. See how he like it."

Vanka was quiet.

"It's not like he ain't gonna get his truck back," Amber said. "Might take a couple days, but once we dump it, the police gonna get it for him. That's what they do. We might even be doing him a favor, depending on his insurance."

"What?" Vanka squinted. "He said it's new."

"Exactly. That's how it be with some insurance. I'm serious. That man might make out—if he got the right kind of insurance." Amber was absorbed, examining the wavy-gravy polish on her thumbnail. "Anyway"—she looked up again—"what you worried about him for? He got money. Wouldn't have no truck like that, if he didn't."

They were quiet.

"He ain't suspicious, is he?" Amber asked.

"I don't know what he is," Vanka said. "He'd be cool if you hadn't zapped out on him."

"I can't help it. That man made me mad."

"Whatever," Vanka said. "You gonna have to squash it now."

"You're right," Amber said. "Soon as I finish this game of pool, he's gonna see how nice I can be."

They were quiet.

"Something ain't right about this," Vanka said.

"What you mean?"

"I don't know. I got a funny feeling."

"Like what?"

"Like we shoulda stayed home."

On the muted post-game show, Magic Johnson's hands pantomimed.

Vanka swiveled to check on Amber in the poolroom and listed on the stool. The floor seemed to give out. She caught herself, two hands on the bar, and was good again.

The man saw it all. A throb of pity went through him. She was very drunk—*sozzled* was the word he'd heard as a small boy. Something about the tottering girl had brought the word back to him and given away her youth. She was just a kid; he'd seen it; then it was gone; then back again. Kind of spooky, but he had seen it. He had thought maybe eighteen, nineteen. Now he realized that that couldn't be true. "How old are you?"

"Nineteen," Vanka lied.

He eased back, a scornful tilt—"Sheee. If that ain't somebody's shinola"—and pushed away his beer. "Your friend nineteen too?"

All at once he felt a little raunchy for liking the way her tank top rode up her back showing the pink elastic of her drawers under low-slung shorts. He glanced at the door, then pulled over a menu and slid it towards her. "Let's get you something to eat. You wanna a hamburger?"

She looked at the man's tan, spongy face, and opened the laminated menu. The words see-sawed. "They got cheeseburgers?"

"I'm pretty sure they do."

"I'll take a cheeseburger."

"Alright."

"I like mine with a lot of pickles."

"Your friend gonna eat?" he asked. "Or is she gone?"

"She's still playing pool. She'll probably take some chicken fingers."

He nodded and then caught the bartender's eye and ordered the food. "You seem like you oughta be home in bed, cupcake."

"What do you know about it?" Her speech was still crisp; it was her head.

"I look at the news," the man said.

"They don't know anything—'cept what's already over and done."

The man watched her eyes, which were so blue and fragile they looked lit from behind. "What're you scared of in this world?"

The question irritated the girl. "Nothing. I ain't scared of nothing."

"Nothing? Not even goblins? Everyone's scared of those."

"I don't know what those are."

"Then you're a lucky girl. A pretty girl with luck. Can't do better than that."

She squinted at him. "I don't feel lucky."

"No one ever does," he said. "Not till it's felled off. Then you realize what you had."

She tried to think about that, to see if it was true, but she couldn't make a picture of all the pieces.

"How about bats or spiders?" he asked.

"I don't like bats, but that don't mean I'm scared of 'em."

They were quiet.

"I used to be scared of people," Vanka said, "scared to look at them anyway."

"Why?" he asked.

"I don't know. People always think somebody's looking at them wrong. People are mean, aren't they?"

"They can be," he said. "Some anyway."

They were quiet.

"You got someone at home?"

"Who's asking?" she said.

"Your ride."

"Walking don't bother me," she said. "I done it before."

He jiggled his jaw side-to-side, like it helped him think, and tried another way. "I got a mother down at the bottom of Virginia used to think I was her ashtray till they took me away."

Vanka stifled a cringe.

"How about you?" he asked.

She waited. "We never been to Virginia."

He sipped his beer, giving up.

After a while, their order was slid in front of them. They paused before the plates of hot food. Over Amber's plate, Vanka layered a blanket of overlapping napkins. Then she lifted the bun on her own food and ate several pickle slices before digging in.

"A quick check under the hood never hurts," the man remarked, almost to himself.

She ate quickly. Meanwhile, he unfurled the napkin-wrapped silverware, and took his time. Using his knife and fork, he started on the cheeseburger carefully and methodically. He cut it in neat squares, keeping each little tower of meat and cheese and bun to-gether. After a moment, he was aware that the girl had stopped eating to watch him. He set down the silverware. "You don't like how I eat?" he asked.

"I just never seen no one eat a cheeseburger like that."

"Watch your own food," he said. "It'll taste better that way."

She turned back to her plate. She finished the cheeseburger and began working on the mountain of french fries, eating two or three at a time. After she was done, she swiped a napkin across her mouth and said, "My Mom's Polish. If you're so dying to know." She held up her wrist where the lacy green letters curled like a bracelet.

He sounded it out: "*Warsawa.*"

"I thought my Mom would like it, but I was wrong."

"She cook Polish?" he asked.

"Pierogies," she said. "We get 'em at Safeway. Beside the waffles."

"She's not one of them that's hard to understand, is she?"

"Not to me."

He stabbed a cube of meat. "How's it sound when she talks?"

"It's normal to me. But other people say she sounds funny."

He finished chewing. "Funny like how?"

"Just little things."

He waited.

"She says Burger King*s*."

He liked that. "What else?"

"It's hard to explain. It's something you gotta hear for yourself."

He took a forkful of food and chewed. "I don't plan on introducing myself, so you can go on."

She paused. "*Vould you like a sandvich, sveetie.*"

He smiled at these strange sounds.

"Something else too," Vanka said. "She's got an uncle back there named Sewer. I seen it on letters he wrote. Signed his name Sewer. But they don't say Sewer. They say Se*ver*."

He thought about that. "You speak it too?"

She shook her head.

"Nothing? Not even bless you or good night?"

She hesitated. "I know a couple things."

"Such as what?"

"Well, *viervorka* is squirrel. And *tencha* is rainbow. And *kochanie malanka* means dear little one. My Mom still calls me *kochanie*. Even though I'm grown."

"You ain't grown," he said.

"Yes, I am."

"You don't look it."

"Yeah, huh."

"You're still getting bigger, ain't you?"

"I don't know," Vanka said.

He looked away. "Don't look like you done blooming to me, anyway."

The bar had begun to empty out. He withdrew a clip from his pocket and peeled off six twenties and set them on the bar. Her eyes flashed to the ruffled green bills and looked away. "Lemme go find her," Vanka said, and stood.

Before the arched opening to the poolroom, Vanka heard Amber, bragging on herself, joking somebody.

Bent over the green felt, a dread-head white boy in breakaway sweatpants sighted his stroke.

"I'm about to eat your food," Vanka said.

Amber wheeled, her face brightening. "What food?"

The boy shot and missed.

"It's a whole plate of chicken fingers that's yours."

Amber shook her head pitifully. "You must've teased him something terrible." She lifted a celebratory hand, and they hooked pinkies.

The boy looked at Vanka. "What's up?"

"What's up?" Vanka said and turned again to Amber. "Can you come on? He's about to bounce."

"Here I come." Amber circled the pool table. "Soon as I prove Yo can't bang with me."

Back at the bar, Vanka sat again. "She's coming."

"Hor-ray," the man said.

Vanka took up a nickel from the change on the bar and spun it. "I don't know why'd you come all the way to this country to clean office buildings every night. Coulda done that back in Poland."

He was quiet.

She looked at her phone. It was late. "It's hard on my Mom too. Sometimes she works two jobs to take care of us. Spends half her life on buses, or waiting for them."

"Just you two?"

"Me and my brother, but we don't click like that."

The man waited.

"Thinks he's perfect. He even wants to be a police."

"Is that bad?"

"It's embarrassing."

He was quiet.

"Cops are cruddy. I don't trust 'em. They'll give anyone a badge."

He was quiet, watching her.

"What about you?" he asked.

"Me?" She was holding up the back of her fork, trying to see herself in the tines. "I need to chill out. Sometimes you can forget who you are—like it's not even you doing all this crazy stuff, but someone else."

He listened.

"Anyway, I'm quite sure this world's gonna spin just fine when I ain't in it."

He screwed up his face. "Who's gonna feed the cats?"

"I used to didn't," she said. "They must've known how to get their own food once."

He looked at her. "You know what mooses eat?"

"Mooses?" she said, trying to picture one.

"Yeah, mooses."

"What?"

"Bark."

"Bark?" she asked. "Like on a tree?"

"That bark."

She laughed. "That's stupid."

"It's the truth."

They were quiet.

"We got any mooses around here?" she asked.

"You gotta go to Canada."

"Have you?"

"I lived there once."

She tried to picture what Canada might be like, but all she saw in her mind were reindeer pulling a sled though the sky.

"Was it what you thought it would be?" Vanka asked.

The question struck him as strange. "Was alright," he said. "If you don't mind composting dead deer for the highway bureau."

"Yuck," Vanka said.

It was then that Amber sauntered back to the bar. She stood beside him, as if presenting herself. The man regarded the moody girl who had turned on him. Contrition did not come easy to her, but she strove for a tone of sincerity. "I'm sorry for acting stupid." She flattened a palm to her chest and put on an ingratiating smile. "I didn't mean no harm. Things come out wrong sometimes."

He looked at her pretty face—the hazel eyes and soft cheekbones and the sharp, delicate lines of her jaw—all of it made fierce with pride. Her words sounded empty, rehearsed even. He had an idea that in making a sad play for his sympathy, the girl had lowered herself and it was up to him to spare her anymore humiliation. He inclined his head and gave her a forgiving, "You're alright."

Her relief was real. "You could've laughed at that man on my phone," Amber said. "You took it too serious."

"You should watch out for men that expose themselves."

She gave him a couple broken chuckles and extended a hand. "Squashed?"

Her hand felt small in his.

Vanka pushed the plate of chicken fingers towards her. "Here," she said, "these yours."

The food was cold by then, but Amber was hungry and took two quick bites. "These good," Amber said, dipping the breaded chicken in the little tin tub of honey mustard. "Appreciate it."

They were quiet.

"What you all been talking about, anyway?" Amber asked.

"Canada," Vanka said.

"Canada?" Amber's face recoiled. "Why?"

Vanka flicked her eyes at the man. "He lived there."

Confusion knotted Amber's brows and faded. "I know your gas bill was high. Even the word sounds cold."

Vanka was watching herself in the bar mirror. "Bet you're still you, even in Canada."

"I don't even know what that means, sweetheart," he said.

For a moment it had seemed like it was not really her in the mirror. She shut her eyes and opened them again. It had been exciting to take the other cars, and there'd been so many they kind of mixed together. A lot of the men had deserved it. They'd been pervs or nasty old men who couldn't keep their hands to themselves and Vanka and Amber had invented wild lies to tell them. Everything she'd told this man tonight had been true, and although the idea of leaving him without his truck seemed wrong, it also felt like things had already been set in motion, and there wouldn't be any bringing them back now.

"I should shut up," Vanka said.

Back in the man's truck, Amber took up the same spot in the middle. The radio was still tuned to 92 Q, though lower.

"I'ma need a cigarillo. Can we stop, please?" Amber asked. "There's a gas station up the hill. They got the apple cider flavor."

The man nodded, and they rode along.

Another minute and he was turning into the gas station, curling around the pumps to a far corner. When he slid between the parking stripes, Amber dug three singles out of her bra. "I got money," she said, "but they won't sell 'em to me. Say you gotta be twenty-one."

He ignored the money and shifted into park.

"Please don't leave us in here with no music and no air," Amber said. "We'll burn up out here."

"It ain't that hot," he said and elbowed open the door of the idling truck. The girls listened to his clacking boots on the pavement and watched him enter the store, clocking him. Then Amber craned around, surveying the pump islands behind and to their left. A yellow Stanley Steemer van was filling up, its driver, a carpet cleaner in a beige work shirt, stood over the nozzle. Amber read aloud the saloon style lettering on the van's side, "hot water extraction for deep cleaning."

Inside the glassed-in mini-mart, the man waited behind another customer. Amber watched him peering down at the cheeses and meats in the deli case. She readied herself, her eyes following his hands, waiting for the transaction that would occupy him. When he got to the cashier and pointed at the cigarillos on the rack, Amber slid behind the wheel. Everything happened fast now: she tapped a foot on the brake, slipped the shift down a notch into reverse, and, almost innocently, drifted backwards. Then she cranked over the wheel, threw it in drive, and gunned the engine. The machine shot forward so violently the girls felt struck from behind.

Though it was not a sound the man associated with his truck, he turned to it. For a moment, he thought the truck's wild arc would take out a gas pump. But Amber stomped two feet on the brake and the truck shuddered down in a heeling pitch. They had clipped the lip of a pump island and now, just clear of the hoses, straddled it.

The man was out of the mini-mart, already in a dead sprint.

The girls pulled themselves upright and saw him, making up ground fast. The accelerator plunged again, and the tires chirped and kicked free. Under them, humped fuel lids rocked and rattled as the truck skittered across the lot.

The man was measuring their path, closing, his ponytail bobbing. Then he realized he'd be run down by his own truck if he didn't let up. He broke off into a loping stride and, in a motion made lazy with resignation, threw the cigarillos at the Ford's side panel.

Amber was yelling, wagging a finger at him. "You know you weren't supposed to be with no girls this young!"

Vanka felt his pearl gray eyes slide past. She slunk down, shrinking.

He watched the boxed, red taillights on his Ford disappearing and swore. Then he whirled to the carpet cleaner, who clapped the hose nozzle on its hook, and waved him over. "C'mon."

Out on the street, Amber drove average, neither faster, nor slower than other cars on the road. She adjusted the mirrors and picked at the rolled hem on her shorts, which felt cinched around the crotch. "Why they always got the same dumb look on their faces?" Amber said.

Vanka straightened, looking back. "He was alright."

"Whatever," Amber said.

"No seriously, he didn't even wanna do nothing. I could tell."

"Just spending his money on conversation, huh?" Amber said. "Please."

It wasn't long before Amber saw it: something in the rearview mirror that did not fit the pace of paired headlights it zigzagged through. "What is that?" she said, even as she knew. "Can't be no police already."

Vanka whipped around to look, and the yellow van slid in behind them. Over the bright halo lights and the chromed snout of the Stanley Steemer, Vanka was sure she saw the man's vengeful glare in the passenger seat.

"It'd be like him to do some dumb shit like this," Amber said.

Now the Stanley Steemer's high beams strobed and its flashers flashed, and the driver banged out a frantic plea on the horn.

It had not happened this way before, but Amber felt ready. At the next corner she snatched the wheel wickedly left, and they leaned with it.

The van stayed with them. Ahead, the red lights were lined up on Eastern Avenue. Timed that way, to keep late-night drivers idling at each block. Amber drew herself over the wheel, gripping hard, and opened it up. The engine whined as they blew through one red light, then another, still accelerating, the red dots seeming to smear together.

At this reckless display, the Stanley Steamer hung back, unsure, and then, as if shocked dumb, stopped altogether, right there in the middle of Eastern Avenue.

Amber took the ramp to 83, a winding elevated expressway which twisted north out of downtown. They were climbing. Above the tree tops, the road pitched one way and then the other, the white jersey wall at their side ripping past like a ragged stitch.

Vanka slouched back, squeezed closed her eyes, tucked into herself. She was home then, in her room, the zebra print bedspread, staring at the collage of Drake she pinned on the wall, the creak of the oven door and the smell of blintzes—butter and jam and powdered sugar. Then it was sixth grade when she'd been on the Green Team and could talk about clean energy better than most adults, her father punching out the glass on the back door after they'd locked him out, but he was getting in, he was getting in, he was getting—cat make-up for Halloween one year, a floating somersault on a trampoline, something on the weather channel about the Coriolis effect, the saucer-warble of those fuel lids and the man's pearl gray eyes.

Off to the side, buildings flew by—balconied condos, flat-roofed, neon strip malls, row houses capped with slate turrets. But Vanka caught only glimpses, a blur really, the world already tumbling around her.

C armen had been scared to tell Ant about the baby. They were upstairs at his Uncle Byrd's lying on Ant's mattress under the window.

"We made a baby?" Ant stood.

She hushed him. "Shhh, people gonna hear you."

"Look at your little booty." His thumb and middle finger formed a cuff over her slender arm. "How you gonna have a baby?"

"Stop." She was not smiling, and her eyes were wet.

He sat again, thumbing a streak from her cheek. "What is this? What you doing?"

"Telling you makes it realer."

"I got you," he said. "I'ma be there for you."

"You don't even know what you're saying yet."

He reached into his backpack and held up a CD case Sharpied in graffiti lettering: *Veri: Truth from the Trenches.*

"Don't nobody want your mix tape, Ant."

"You don't think so?" The window was sticky with humidity, and he fought to lift it. "A lot of people gonna wish they were me." He sat and tore a sheet of geometry homework from his notebook and let out a long breath. "You must don't want me to be happy," he said.

"I'm trying to be realistic, and you're talking about some mix tape nobody's ever heard of."

Downstairs laughter broke out. Uncle Byrd called himself a tattoo artist, but most of the time Carmen was there, it looked like a house party: a regular crew of old heads, arguing over spades or tunk, bumping 70s slow jams on a record player—the only working one Carmen had ever actually seen.

From the mattress, Carmen looked up at the flaking eaves and the blue sky above. She pinched her t-shirt collar and flapped it. "Dag, ain't no air in here."

Ant stood and shimmied half out the window. He picked a green clover from the tarred porch roof below. On the mattress, he lay on his stomach and twirled it under her chin.

"You're stupid." She giggled. "I was afraid you'd be mad."

"A baby only makes you mad if you don't love the person."

"I didn't want you to blame me for something"—

"For what? It's not even like that."

"I don't know. It's just gonna be a lot on us."

"We'll be alright." He looked at her belly. "We'll do it together."

"My mother's gonna have a fit too."

He shrugged. "She can't stay mad forever."

Ant walked two fingertips over each of the copper freckles high on Carmen's cheeks. "Pitter patter, pitter patter," he said, as he went along. "I been talking to the counselor at school and I'm gonna get my CDL after I graduate."

She liked this. "Okay, what you gonna drive?"

"I'm not for sure, but the counselor's got the connect at Lincoln Tech."

"Don't they go all over the country, those drivers?"

"Yeah, but you come back. You might be gone a couple days, then you come home. And the money's right."

Carmen looked at the ceiling above the missing acoustic tiles where the room had been blue once, and beige after that, and she allowed herself to think about the kind of life they might have.

He pulled her flat on to his stomach and tugged down the elastic waist on her shorts.

"Why you always in my drawers?" she asked.

"Why you always in mine?"

She held his face in her hands, studying it. He had a long face, a straight nose, wavy hair, and secret-sweet eyes like something was always about to be funny. They were the same smiling eyes she'd first noticed in sixth grade after his poem had won the Enoch Pratt contest and for a month his rhymes rode the sides of all the buses: *The two-faced weather, tickle like a feather, cracking like mama's belt leather.*

"The baby might get your pretty eyes," she said.

"Might get your freckles."

"Might get your soft hair."

"Of course the baby gonna get that."

"Hope the baby don't get your teeth," she said. "They're real jacked up."

"So now you gonna crack on my teeth?"

"Lemme see." He tasted like gumballs, fruity and sweet. "You're good."

"Thought so," he said.

"That day, when it happened—they'd closed school 'cause of the snow and we stayed in bed watching that movie with Denzel"—

"*American Gangster.*"

"Yeah, that day," she said, "I knew we'd made a baby."

"How?" he asked.

"I don't know. Some things. You can just feel."

They were quiet.

"I'm glad it's you," he said.

"What you mean? Who else would it be?"

"Not like that. I just wouldn't want no baby with no other girl."

The trouble started on a Friday in the cafeteria. Carmen sat across from Ant at a long lunch table under the fluorescent grid. The air was steamy with a starched gravy smell. Around them, kids sat eating or talking at other tables, the babble of all their voices climbing over each other. Carmen ate franks and beans off a Styrofoam tray.

"Why are you giving my baby that nasty food?" Ant asked.

"It's good." She offered him a sporkful.

He'd eaten his pizza to the crust, and now he pointed it at her. "Pythagorus said beans ain't right."

"Who's that?"

He tapped the last drops of punch from the carton into his mouth. "You need to start going to math more."

"Not when they keep putting letters in it."

Ant stood and crossed the room. She watched him drag a hand along the slatted rails to the lunch lady. This was when Valdez came over to their table. Still in eleventh grade, Valdez Fleming was the best player on a team of good ball players: a hellified scorer with a slick handle. Recruiters were still coming out for his spring rec league games, saying he might go Division I. A broad forehead, a face of smooth clay, Valdez wore Adidas headbands and Adidas shorts that showed great blocks of muscle below his knees. He bragged about hotel parties and the hook-up he already had at the Mondawmin Foot Locker.

Valdez swiveled a plastic bucket chair backwards and planted his elbows on the table. The chair seemed too small for him. "So when you gonna let me get that?" His eyes lingered below her belly, and he had brought with him a smell of Axe body spray.

"I'm not." She chewed her food.

He sat his chin on his long forearm, fake hurt. "But I thought we're cool."

"I'm cool with a lot of people. That doesn't mean"—

"But I'm special."

"So am I."

He sighed.

It was May and a breeze snuck through the courtyard windows and she'd gotten her hair done in fish-scale braids and in her crop top she knew she looked good. "Too bad, too, because you would love it," she said.

Valdez bit his knuckles and winced. "You must be trying to hurt me."

This was when Ant returned, one hand holding two small punch cartons.

Valdez spoke without looking up. "What's up, playa?"

"What's up."

Valdez inched closer to Carmen. "I thought that was your girl."

Ant's eyes stayed on Valdez while he unsealed a carton.

"She don't sound like she claim you no more, bruh," Valdez said.

"Don't do that," she said. "Don't lie on yourself."

"Now you wanna act funny." Valdez sucked his teeth. "Just 'cause he here."

"You in the wrong spot, Yo," Ant said. "The dick riders back at your table."

Valdez let himself collapse into Carmen, laughing. "Yo taking it hard."

Ant tugged up his jeans. "I'm not for a whole lotta back and forth."

When he started around the table, Valdez also rose. Ant was not small, but beside Valdez he seemed smaller. They were very close and Ant's eyes were flat and empty, like he was looking at nothing at all.

Then the cafeteria monitor, a swatch of trash liners in his hand, had gotten between them. It was too late, though, because they both had their hard faces on, adding more words to the ones that would not be taken back.

By evening, it had gone from talk at school, to talk on Facebook and Instagram, to texts popping up on Ant's phone.

"Yo," Ant said, drawing it out.

Carmen grabbed his phone: *Lil boys get hurt coming out their lane.*

She scrolled and read another: *His girl gonna be boo-hooing when he get got.*

"Who is Basic?" she asked.

"One of his little crew. That boy with the idiot cackle in World History."

"Always got on a different Polo?"

Ant nodded.

"I can't believe they really doing all this," she said.

"They got that man's head pumped up. Think he gonna do anything now."

"Something wrong with Valdez."

Ant stood at the window in his navy boxers. "Them people getting killed down on Fulton? That's their crew doing that."

"Who?"

"All them. Valdez. Basic. That other boy that's always around them."

She was confused. "Fulton?"

He turned back to her and, though his mouth was closed, she could see his tongue sweep across his front teeth, over and back. "They stepped on somebody's strip down there."

"That ain't got nothing to do with you," she said. "You ain't a dope boy."

"You don't think they gonna be in it now?" He had turned away again. "You don't think I gotta think about that?"

She sat on her heels and watched the muscles in his shoulders, which were wide without being bulky. "This is fucked up," Carmen said.

He went out in the hall and she heard him go in the bathroom and the knock of the toilet seat going up and pee splashing in the bowl. She listened to his hands swishing under the sink faucet. After a while, the splatter of water smoothed into an unbroken hiss. She followed the sound down the hall. Ant was kneeling, his hands in the cabinet under the sink, and she knew what he was doing. This was where Uncle Byrd kept one of his guns: a black Hi-Point .38 wrapped in a washcloth tucked in an SOS soap pad box. When Ant rose, he saw that she'd been watching.

"What?" He shut off the water.

"You need to chill."

"I ain't doing nothing."

She caught hold of his jaw. "I don't know what you're thinking, but you better leave it alone."

He twisted free. "And they better hope they're all talk. Because I got something for 'em."

"It's not that serious."

"I'm not inside none of their heads. I can't tell you what they gonna do."

"Can you stop?"

"And if he think I'm one of those gonna stay hid, he got that wrong too." He was walking back to the bedroom.

She followed. "Can you just stop?"

He checked his phone again and tossed it on the bed. He went back to the window and stood looking down at the street.

"Just calm down."

His nostrils pinched with the air he pulled in.

"Think about something else. Play the game"—she tipped her face at the Play Station on the dresser—"clean your tennies. Is that so hard?"

"My sneakers aren't dirty."

"I'm sure you'll find something on them."

"I'ma be cool."

"I don't believe you," she said. "You wouldn't be like this if you were."

"Like what?"

"Like you can barely get your words out."

They were quiet.

"You won't even look at me," she said.

He drew a breath and turned to her. "They got a word for that."

"What, heated?"

"Brooding."

"Brooding? Sounds weird."

He sat. "A lot of words like that. At first anyway."

"I'm gonna talk to Valdez," she said. "Tell him it's squashed."

A smile flickered and vanished in a sigh. "It ain't about you no more."

"This is stupid." She slapped her knuckles into her palm.

"I'm alright. I ain't worried about them. Long as his little crew don't try nothing, I'ma be cool." His eyes looked dim, somewhere else.

"I don't want nothing bad to happen," she said.

"Nothing bad gonna happen."

Carmen took his hand. She liked his long, delicate fingers and his nails, which were broad and flat. She looked at his fingers now, so slack in hers they were hardly there at all.

After school, they walked together to the bus stop. A pewter MTA bus idled on the skirt of brick that ran along the gutter. The bus was choked with students. Kids pressed forward. Not everyone was going to fit, and no one looked like they wanted to wait for the next one. Across the street, a mattress man hollered, "Kings and queens!" from a box truck. Then, dipping a shoulder, Valdez bobbed out of the crowd. Golds behind a twisted sneer, gold links hanging over his v-neck tee, he came on.

Behind him, moving with him, the boy they called Basic, and two drowsy-faced dudes too old to be students.

The gun was out from Ant's dip and, for an instant, he held it low and swingy.

The shots kicked up through Ant's arm fast and steady. They chopped at Valdez and carried him back. The sulfured smoke, the banging in Carmen's ears, and the flashing jolts coming off Ant's hand, all mixed together.

Valdez was down, alone on his back, moaning, fists locked, head flopping side to side, knee up, knee down beside a book bag somebody had dropped. Blood pooled at his hip and blotted his grey drawstring shorts.

Everyone had broke. The bus heaved off, coiling exhaust.

Carmen turned to Ant, but he was gone too.

When she couldn't run anymore, she jog-walked. She stopped and clasped her knees. Something hot rushed up her throat, stinging. The Cup of Noodles she'd had for lunch spattered her white Nikes.

"You alright, sweetie?" a man asked.

She straightened, spat, drew a wrist across her mouth and moved on. Her ears still rang, and her mouth tasted acid. She hurried a prayer, fingers fumbling over her phone. Sunlight knifed off the screen, and she cupped it, tilting it one way and another. Ant did not answer and no circles bubbled back from the texts she sent. Sirens sounded nearby. She slipped into an alley and draped her forearms on a loading dock.

A man, laid out and ponchoed in dark plastic bags, stirred on a wooden pallet. She tried Ant again. Across the alley, flies buzzed over white buckets of cooking oil behind a carry-out. Then she made herself stop trying, believing this upped the chances of him answering.

She brushed grit from her forearms and went on to North Avenue where she used her bus pass to catch the 13 to Walbrook Junction. At Uncle Byrd's, the police were already there.

Four cruisers parked any kind of way, the front door wide open, a louvered window shutter knocked loose and hanging crooked.

At the Inner Harbor, she found a bench. Gulls circled, cawed, dipped and rose again. A ball game was starting and fans, most of them white, moved past in Orioles gear. Some got in line to buy pennants or hats from vendors under orange tents hung with black bunting.

It was already all over her phone. Valdez was getting all the love, like he was the good one in this; other people—some she didn't even know—spat slurs, blaming Carmen.

She set the screen face down and clasped her hands between her knees and tried to settle herself. She took deep breaths for the baby, believing it would help them both.

Her memories of the afternoon were scattered. Of course, she remembered a lot, but some of it, about getting to Uncle Byrd's or here, was patchy. Her mind shuffled the images, ordering them, working to fill holes, returning each time to Valdez twisting on the ground in his blood. She saw again the ribbon of students peeling off from the bus stop, frantic and getting in each other's way. She wondered if Valdez was dead now. It didn't seem like he could be. She held her stomach and hoped not.

Her mother was a nurse's aide at Sunnyvale and by now she'd be at work, feeding or diapering old folks. And soon, the police would be at their house, if they weren't already. Carmen tapped her mother's number and let it ring.

"Ma," Carmen said, her voice shaky. "Something happened."

It was dusk and there were no shadows, but Carmen could smell the pollen coating the cars parked on her street.

Her mom had spent thirty dollars to Uber home from Hunt Valley and she was waiting at the door, still in her turquoise scrubs. Inside, she squeezed Carmen close and for a long while said nothing at all. Then, she held Carmen square in front of her. "I told you about that boy. Outa all the ones you could've picked."

"That's not true," Carmen said. "Ant's low key. He don't bother no one."

"Nothing's been right since you started with him. Now this."

"They were plotting on him. He was in fear for his life being tooken."

A banging on the front door, abrupt and heavy, startled them. Carmen went to the sunroom. Over her mother's potted plants, she saw through the windows, two police, standing at the top of their steps under the porch light. Except for the shiny badges that hung on lanyards over Kevlar vests, these knockers could've been anybody.

Her mother unbolted the door and tugged it open.

"I'm Detective Pritchard."

Carmen was not looking at him. Her eyes were on the other's burly, white neck where a green spider was tattooed on a red web. He had a blond stubble that caught salt-white flakes from his acne.

Knockers always made themselves look ratchet, but Carmen said it anyway. "You all don't look like no police."

Pritchard was much older, creased about the eyes and mouth. They say black don't crack, Carmen thought, but he had. He held up a picture of Carmen the school used for her student ID, comparing the photo to the girl. "You heard from Anthony?"

"Nobody calls him that."

"Then Ant," the one with the spider said. "You hear from Ant?" He was chomping gum too fast, staring hard at the empty foyer behind them, one hand on the butt of his holstered gun, swaying restlessly in his Tims.

"No."

"Mind if we check inside?" Spider asked.

"Yes, I do mind," her mother said.

"You can either let us check now, or we'll get the warrant."

"Get the warrant then," her mother said.

"Once we get the warrant, we won't be coming in nice. You're not going to like how we leave your place." Pritchard sounded like he cared.

"I got insurance," her mother said.

"Still, I would hate for you to have to come behind us."

Carmen had seen how police tear up people's houses, just to be cruddy. Her Mom was already stressed. She didn't need the police trashing her house. Maybe, if they let them check now, they might be satisfied, then go away and leave them alone. "Let 'em look, Ma."

Her mother sucked in her cheeks, watching them, and then she stepped aside. "Go on ahead."

Mother and daughter were made to go to the bottom of the steps where they stood on the sidewalk. When the detectives went through her door, they went with guns out. "Good Lord," her mother whispered.

They took their time. Once Carmen saw Pritchard in her mother's bedroom window upstairs.

After they finished, the four of them stood again outside.

"Go in the house now, Carmen," her mother said.

"We're not done," Pritchard said. "Stay right here."

"You all wanted to check my house. I let you. I think that's enough."

"We'll tell you what's enough," Pritchard said.

They watched him.

"It's a school shooting. Look at the news. It's not going away." Pritchard turned to Carmen. "You had a problem with Valdez?"

"What happened to Valdez?"

"Your boy shot him up is what happened."

Her stomach fluttered. "Not my boyfriend."

"Put three hot ones in that young man."

She swallowed. "I think y'all confused."

Her mother stiffened beside her daughter's lies. "Whatever that boy has done, is on him," her mother said. "I didn't raise her to be in the streets."

"We could actually lock your daughter up on conspiracy," Spider said.

"For what?" Carmen asked.

"Schools are outfitted with cameras everywhere," Pritchard said. "Outside, inside. High, low. Who did what and when to whom is not in question."

"So?" Carmen's arms crossed defiantly, like this didn't mean what he thought it did.

"And you know who else in that camera, don't you?" Spider asked.

Her mother stared at him.

"It's here, on my phone." Pritchard held the screen before her and touched her elbow, as if this would be a hard thing they would do together.

The video played and after a moment her mother reached out and flattened her hand over the screen and seemed to steady herself. "When you lock that boy up, it'll be the best thing for us."

"Eff that," Carmen said. "You're not supposed to take their side and be with them like that."

Her mother removed her glasses and pinched between her brows. "That sounds just like that boy too. You get that from Ant?"

"Ain't no Ant nothing. That's a bad look for anyone."

"We're not criminals." She fixed her eyes on Carmen. "And I'm not gonna live like one."

"He got a right to protect himself, don't he? Or is he just supposed to let them do whatever?"

"Did you know Ant was armed?" Pritchard interrupted.

Carmen had wrapped her arms around her stomach, and she did not answer.

"Speak," her mother ordered. "So they can get what they need and leave us be."

Carmen watched Pritchard and shook her head. In his camouflage shorts, and turned-around ball cap, a gold stud shining in one ear, Pritchard was neat and steady, even if he did look old. "Did you know Valdez was going to be outside?" Pritchard went on.

"It wasn't just Valdez. He had a bunch of dudes with him."

"But only Valdez got hit."

"I know what everybody else knows. He gonna be taking his game or whatever to Towson or Morgan, wherever he got his scholarship to."

"His playing days are over," Pritchard said. "Found out the doctors had to move his bowel. His pelvis—the bones in his hip—they're all over, in places they shouldn't be. Any *walking* he does will be with a cane."

"That wasn't no spitball your boy was banging off with," Spider said.

Pritchard chuckled sadly. "What do you call that—good luck or bad?"

She didn't understand.

"*Good* 'cause he gonna live," Spider explained, "or *bad* 'cause all his dreams is gone?"

"They were gonna hurt him," Carmen said. "Talking about, *he gonna be a body*. And people hollering one of Valdez's boys already got hella bodies."

"So his fool self thought it'd be a good idea to shoot someone?" her mother said.

Carmen ignored her. "Look on Valdez's Facebook. Look on Snap."

"We've already seen those posts," Pritchard said.

"So go lock them up," Carmen said. "I know it ain't legal to just keep threatening someone like that."

"He could've told someone at school," Pritchard said. "An administrator. A resource officer."

Carmen rolled her eyes. "C'mon. That's dead."

"Didn't have to be."

"When someone keeps threatening your life?" she asked. "Nah, that ain't Ant. That ain't nobody for real. Not nobody round here anyway."

"Could've just thrown hands and let that be the end of it," Spider said.

"Not as deep as they were. Valdez's whole squad was about to mix in."

"You thought Valdez's crew was coming for him before?" Spider snickered, leaving the thought unfinished.

"See?" she said. "That's what they do."

"Then he should've contacted the police," Pritchard said. "How's that for a novel idea?"

"What planet you live on?" She rounded off the first question with a second: "The fuck?"

Her mother hooked Carmen's arm—"Stop embarrassing me"— and let it go.

Carmen shuttered one eye, massaging the back of her arm. "And why's he sound white? And the other sounds black?" She flicked her eyes at Spider.

Pritchard sat stiffly on the short wall beside their steps and bit back a wince. "Forgive me. Some things don't heal right."

Carmen watched him. "What happened to you?"

"Same thing that happened to Valdez." He twisted at the waist, stretching. "Events have a way of rippling out," Pritchard said. "And hurting others who never had all that much to do with any of it. But they can end up wrecked just the same."

"I don't know what that means."

Pritchard stood. "Yes, you do. Now do your mother a solid by telling that boy to call me and help himself before this gets any worse than it already is."

Inside, her mother went through the house, switching on lights. She went down to the basement and came up and checked all the locks on all the windows and all the doors and drew the curtains and tidied any gaps. She stuck her head in closets and behind doors and got on all fours to see under their beds.

When she was done, she faced Carmen. "Give me your phone. And don't leave this house."

Carmen peered out windows, her hand visoring off the light behind her. She sat on the leather sectional in the living room, muting and unmuting Bravo, afraid of the quiet. Some sounds she heard— the lady next door whose pipes rattled the walls when she ran her water, wind in the pin oak out front. Others, she might've only thought she heard.

Except for the soup she spat up earlier, she had not eaten that day, and it occurred to her that, even if she wasn't hungry, she should eat for the baby. Had she forgotten about the baby? She rummaged the cupboard, looking over the boxes of uncooked noodles, boxes of rice—Cajun, Spanish, Pilaf—and canned vegetables. She cranked the lid off a can of tuna and forked it into a glass bowl, stirring in salad oil, wine vinegar, season salt and mayonnaise. Everything sounded too loud.

She forked tuna into the tines of the fork and made herself swallow. She wondered if Ant was hungry, and where he would get his food. Ant was the pickiest eater. Apples made his throat prickly. Cap'n Crunch ate up the roof of his mouth. Shrimp itched his knuckles. His father had drunk bad water in Afghanistan and never come home, and although Ant had few memories of the man, he worried about being poisoned by food or drinks that looked good but weren't.

Ant would know better than to come here, wouldn't he? She didn't think he would risk going to his mother's house either. And what about his clothes—he would not be able to get to them, in the morning, or maybe ever. She checked the weather channel. Clouds and T-storms tomorrow. Had he found some place where he could get inside? If not, would he be inside—somewhere—when the rain came tomorrow?

A siren's clipped squawk startled her. At the window she brushed aside the curtain. A police car had pulled to the curb. An open laptop was mounted on the dash. Its blue glow traced the contours of the console, and the officer behind it. Silently, the cruiser's lights came on, flicking watery reflections on the windows of parked cars.

Carmen ducked upstairs. Her mother was asleep now. She took a folded blanket from the foot of the bed and lay on the dark floor, listening to her mother's breathing. Through the curtain seams the cruiser's lights pulsed the walls and ceiling, yellow-blue-red, yellow-blue-red, yellow-blue-red. She shut her eyes. After a while, the cruiser revved its engine and sped off.

She usually stayed on the phone with Ant until she fell asleep. Stretched on the floor beside her mother's bed, Carmen could do no better than jagged fits of dozing.

Two days later, a boy with a high-top fade and mirrored shades came to the door.

"You're Carmen?"

"Who's asking?"

He looked to the corner. "I need to give you something. It's from Ant. But I'm not doing it out here."

She let him in and closed the door. In the foyer, he dug in his pocket and handed her a fat flip phone.

She took it. "What's this for?"

"What you think?"

"Where is he?"

"I'm not even here so I wouldn't know."

"Please."

He lifted the sunglasses, stood on tiptoes, checking outside the window, then slid the sunglasses down again.

"Lemme get your number," Carmen asked.

"What you need my number for?"

"What if I need to call you?"

"You can't call me."

"Not for nothing bad."

"Not for nothing at all," he said.

"I might have a question."

"Go ahead."

"Is he alright?" she asked.

"Yeah, he's good."

"What if nobody calls it?"

The boy was looking outside. He pulled open the door and lowered his sunglasses. "Then I guess he wasn't that pressed about you after all."

She would have to keep this phone hidden from her mother, but for now she sat and watched it. She wanted to test it with the house phone but was afraid she'd be putting the police on to it if she did.

Her mind drifted to Valdez. She pictured him in a hospital bed, hooked up to baggies and glowing monitors, pinging and dinging.

She wondered what Valdez thought of himself now. Did he regret what he'd done? Do people like Valdez even care when they've made it hard on others? Some people can't see past themselves, and he'd probably already made himself a hero out of it.

She was no longer staring at the phone when it buzzed.

"How you doing?" Ant asked.

"Are you okay?"

"Maintaining. Doing the best I can."

"You're not hurt, are you?"

"No, I'm good."

"I didn't realize none of that was gonna happen," she said.

"Yeah, well, he kept coming, even after he saw what I had. All of them did."

"I keep seeing it, the same thing, like it's stuck in my head."

"Try don't think about it," Ant said.

"I miss you so bad."

"You don't even know," he said.

"Police are on me, heavy."

"You ain't none of their business," Ant said. "Tell 'em try and find me."

"That's what they're doing."

"It's gonna die down after a while. It's just real hot right now."

"I don't know," she said.

"You don't think so?"

"They could be listening right now."

"Let 'em try. Ain't nothing to hear on two trap phones."

"I wanna see you so bad," she said. "Can I? Can I see you?"

"That's just how they're waiting to get me. Let you take them right to me."

"So I can't see you no more?"

"Of course you gonna see me."

"How?" she asked.

"You got any money?"

"Not much. Just the couple dollars my mother gives me here or there."

"Can you get some?"

She thought of the coffee tin where her mother stowed fallback cash in the cupboard. "Maybe," she said. "It's not gonna be a whole lot. What you thinking?"

"I'm not for sure yet."

They were quiet.

"I think I'm about to be showing," she said.

"What?"

"My stomach's gonna be sticking out for real soon."

"Dag, already?" he asked.

"Feels weird."

"You tell your mother?"

"No," she said. "I can't tell her anymore."

"Why?"

She paused. "She's not gonna want me to keep it."

"What you mean?"

"I know my mother. She's not. Not after everything that happened."

"She can't do that."

"It's her house. She can do a whole lot."

"You still gotta tell her, even if she does zap out. You're gonna need her help."

"I don't know," Carmen said. "You might need to come up here and tell her yourself."

"I know she doesn't wanna see me," he said.

"But I do."

"Me too."

"I like being with you."

"It's gonna be like that again."

"Doctor said I can do my sonic gram in a couple weeks."

"You been to the doctor without me?"

"Just on the phone."

"You find out what we're having?" he asked.

"No, they still gotta tell me."

They were quiet.

"How're you living—I mean, surviving?" she asked.

"I'm alright."

"Is it bad?"

"No."

"You wouldn't tell me if it was."

"Just be safe. The both of you."

Her mother went to work and came home and passed between rooms, vigilant and mostly silent. Twice she questioned Carmen about Ant. Each time Carmen denied talking to him, and each time her mother looked at her in a way that meant she did not believe her. Carmen felt herself getting thicker—not just her stomach, but all over—and she stayed more in her room.

On a Sunday Carmen heard kitchen sounds—pans clanging, something whisked in a bowl. She dozed and when she woke there were kitchen smells: roast chicken and her mother's baked macaroni cheese.

At the kitchen table, her mother tonged an ear of corn on to Carmen's plate and slid her the butter dish. "I never wanted to raise you here. I wanted us out in the county somewhere—Pikesville or Randallstown, where the schools are better. So after you were born, I called a real estate agent. It was hard to make that call—my father worked his whole life to leave us something. You know what this agent said?"

Carmen waited.

"'You have a beautiful home, but nobody with any money wants to live here.'"

Carmen peppered her food.

"It wasn't a surprise, really. But it's hard to hear a so-called expert tell you the one thing you've got in this world isn't worth more than a Toyota."

"County people are stuck up anyway," Carmen said.

"Better that than this."

"They got problems in the county too."

"Not like ours."

"I guess I don't notice it anymore. It's just regular to me."

"Well, it's not supposed to be."

They ate in silence.

"You know Ant's mother called me?" her mother said.

Carmen set down her fork.

"She's worried about her son."

"Now her fake self wants to act like she cares. She shoulda been worried about Ant when she had the chance."

Her mother started to say something, then stopped, thinking better of it. "I remember what it's like," she said. "Nothing else to think about, but the boy on your mind, and every time you do, your heart melts all over again."

They were quiet.

"But nobody should have to get on a sidewalk with people who work out their problems like Ant tried to," her mother said.

"It's not that simple."

"It can be as complicated as you want to make it, and it still won't be right."

They were in their car, waiting, when Carmen came out of the clinic and stepped into the rain. Pritchard was in the driver's seat. "Can we ride you home?"

She was all the way down on Madison, thirty minutes by bus from home. That they'd followed her this far spooked her. She hated the rain and would've taken a ride from anyone, but not them. Under an umbrella too small for the sideways weather, she scrunched up her face.

She'd been to the store earlier and a plastic bag of Little Debbies and mini-carrots hung on the umbrella hook near her chin where she clutched some brochures the nurse inside had given her. "I'm good." She thought of the fat phone in her back pocket and fought an urge to turn her hips away from them.

"I didn't know," Pritchard said.

"Didn't know what?"

Pritchard's eyes settled on the brochure in her hand: *Foods your Baby Will Love You for*.

"It's for a friend." She was embarrassed.

"We'll see what they say inside," Spider said.

"You all need to stop. You're doing too much." She hurried along.

They coasted beside her and, as they rolled along, Pritchard talked. "I know what you're doing, baby girl. You're still holding on to pictures of pink ribbons and silk lace and pushing a stroller together. You think—both of you probably think it—that you can help each other. But you can't. Neither one of you can do for the other. That's hard to accept, but it's the stone truth."

She stopped. They stopped. Bits of trash rode a little current in the gutter beside their black tires. A scent of air-freshener drifted from their car—strawberry? Raspberry? Some kind of berry. She looked at them. Pritchard had on a black kufi and rain misted the front. On a corner billboard, beside a stone church, an accident lawyer's long, white face rose. A boot kick of wind came up and the rain rippled in it and her umbrella flapped out and back and the stiff face on the billboard stayed the same.

Across the street a bus waited at a traffic light. It was going the wrong direction, but Carmen broke for it. She ran in a hard diagonal, her feet slapping the wet pavement. In two blocks she'd gotten ahead of it. Either because it was raining or because he was one of those nice bus drivers, the doors shushed open at a red light. She thanked him and collapsed her umbrella and when she struggled to tear a ticket from the student passbook, he waved her past.

Her white jeans, splattered and soaked, had begun to chafe and she heard squishing in her Nikes. At an empty seat, she knelt into the window. She rubbed an elbow over the smudged hair grease and pressed her wet face to the glass. The billboard where she'd left them was out of view. She sank into the seat. She didn't think they'd follow the bus. That wasn't them. They preferred popping up out of nowhere, just to get in your head, then go away again till next time.

Ant was on the phone.

Carmen had certain things she'd wanted to ask and now she could not remember what they were. "Have you been thinking of me?"

"All the time."

"I want it to be like it was." She'd crept inside her closet and pressed her face against a coat so her mother would not hear.

"We didn't know how good we had it, did we?" he asked.

"Do you think it'll be like that for us again?"

"A lot of things not how they were. A lot of things I don't know about anymore."

They were quiet.

"I caught myself wondering if you're about ready to give up on us," he said, "like you're ashamed of what I'd done and just don't want to say it."

"You gone crazy, boy," Carmen said. "When the chips is down, we take care of each other."

"I can't go back or rewind it. I can't change nothing that happened. But I never wanted to shoot that boy."

"I know that," she said.

"Valdez's a jerk, but I got some of the same in me."

"You're not like Valdez at all."

"All that pride and neither one of us got nothing to show for it."

In the dark closet, she shifted a foot out of the seam of light.

"I Googled my name and saw myself on the news," Ant said. "They got my picture and everything. I know what people watching their TV's must be thinking: Gangsta. Hardhead. Hoodlum. Headcase. Lost Cause."

"It's a girl," she said.

"What?"

"The baby, it's a girl."

"Oh, man. A girl. For real? That's beautiful."

"I thought you wanted a boy."

"That was before you told me we're having a girl."

"So you're not disappointed?" she asked.

"That's not even a question."

She smiled to herself.

"A girl with my girl," he said. "That's something."

They were quiet.

"You thought of any names?" he asked.

"Not yet. Waiting on you to help me decide. What you think?"

He paused. "Miracle."

"Miracle?"

"You like it?" he asked.

"I never thought of a name like that."

"It come to me that way."

She woke to Ant's voice, but it was only in her head. The pigeons cooed on the sill outside, and she lay listening to their strange songs. She yearned to get the house—some place—ready for the baby. A little bump was showing now and she touched there, looking for signs of something moving.

She stepped into her flip-flops and started for the store still in her plaid pajama bottoms and a drapey tee-shirt.

Spider was already posted-up beside their car before she broke that first corner. She slowed, watching him, then kept on, getting closer. Pritchard got out and came around and stood before her.

"You know he reads the dictionary?" she asked. "Plays Scrabble on his phone too. That's how he knows so many words. Some words, like regular everyday words, he got a special way of adding to them."

They listened.

"He doesn't just say broom; he might say whiskbroom. A pothole? He'll call it a crumble pot."

"Crumble pot?" Pritchard mused.

"Makes sense," Spider said.

She went on. "You know he knows the names of stars? He had a book on it from the library. He's not even half-particular about what he reads."

They listened, letting her go.

"He just notice a lot—way more than me." Her eyes fell to their car where a new chrome bumper shone under an ugly crimp in the hood. She looked up as if remembering something. "Did you know he stays on top of his classes?" she asked. "Keeps up his grades?"

"Evidently, his disposition can change quickly," Pritchard said.

They waited and when she didn't say more, Spider spoke. "That'll make his time pass quicker." He sounded nice now. "It'll help him."

She watched him.

"For real," Spider said. "If he's a reader and he can learn and continue to develop himself, he can handle the time. People like that, sometimes, they come out better."

She felt herself weakened by his appeals and laughed at herself. "Don't put the Sunday comics in front of him. He'll die laughing at *Garfield* and what's the other one with the dog—Snoopy?"

"*Peanuts*," Pritchard corrected.

"Same thing," Carmen said.

"The thing about it, he's not just gonna vanish," Spider went on. "Not with the technology out here now. And there ain't but so many rocks to hide under. Even big brother's got a big brother."

Up the hill, church spires spun clouds to whorled puffs. "I guess Valdez thought he was gonna scare Ant, and Ant was just gonna lay down," she said. "Sometimes I wish he would've."

"I can't blame Ant for staying ready," Spider said. "Not once you factor how crazy it is out here, I can't." He dug grime from under his thumbnail. "I'm not supposed to say that."

She watched him.

"He's got no priors. Still a minor. He might get ten years. Do three. What—that would put him at twenty. Plenty of time left to help raise your child together." Spider smiled at his own sweet logic. "Remember, it's *'tempt* murder, not murder. He didn't kill anyone, right?"

Everything he said sounded good, and she let the idea linger in her mind, believing it could be so. But she caught herself. "You're the *defectives.*" She crushed a tear with a knuckle. "You figure it out."

She opened dresser drawers and touched the things she would have to leave behind: t-shirts and socks, bras and underwear, shorts and jeans. Ant had said they could take no more than could fit in her pockets after he had told her the number of the Greyhound backwards because saying numbers out your mouth can jinx them. She chose a tiny bottle of Miss Dior perfume and the vitamins a nurse at the clinic had given her.

In the hall, she stopped at her mother's doorway and turned the glass knob and stepped in. The bed was neatly made and reflected in the mirror. On the dresser, a short, stained-glass lamp stood near her mother's jewelry chest. One velvet-red drawer was tipped open. It held chunky jade stones and a tarnished gold locket. She'd stood alone in her mother's bedroom many times, soaking up the feeling of being near her mother's things, which had not changed much over the years, and Carmen knew she'd remember this time before all the others.

Outside, she checked for their Crown Vic everywhere, glancing over her shoulder, trying to see around corners. She watched for shadows in the gray light of doorways and sought to pick them out of the faces she came upon. Somewhere, she'd seen a story about drones. She wondered if they had those. Her eyes swept rooftops and when she saw no drones, she looked straight into the sky.

igh-rises, like towers made out of sidewalk. The minute they started talking about blowing us up, we forgot everything we didn't like about Freedom House Projects. No one cared anymore about the spent lights, or some-timey hot water, or the elevator-jamming hustlers. Pretty soon, graffiti cried through stairwells and across doors: Save Freedom House.

          I had a job at a seafood restaurant called Barnacle Bob's. He'd hired me as a dishwasher. Straight away, though, he put me on his boat, working the crab pots. Out there, with the wind popsicling my bones and the boat tossing my stomach, I wanted to tell him to kick rocks. 'Cept then I would've been right back in the house with Excuse. So five, six days a week I hit that first empty #11 and rode the flickering lights down to the harbor where the streets were made of stone. Barnacle Bob was this old crusty dude with a fat face and a yellow beard and a really dirty hat that he called lucky even when it wasn't and he would be there waiting in the dark by the water.

Huddled down, chopping across that bay, gulls at our side, you couldn't help some days from praying those pots come up light. But

Barnacle Bob had taken a chance on me, so I worked to keep his chains snubbed, the slack out of those cleats, his gaffs holstered, his ice iced, and everything else he wanted.

One day after work, I got off the elevator and I could see, way down at the other end, the little girl who lived across the hall, sitting on the floor, locked out, again. She was nine with a Mom probably wronger than mine. J. Cole was rocking in my headphones and the long smooth hallway smelled like old mop and fried onions. I slipped off the headphones and stepped lightly, listening. I pictured the floor see-sawing, then dropping away. In my stomach I could feel how it'd be: all of us on seven kind of lifted together like wishes off a dandelion: Old Leopold practicing trumpet in ran-down Adidas and alligator pajamas, still pretending like he ain't heard the news, that little boy Lopez tapping a soccer ball off his heel like it's on a leash, Ms. B carrying around an old Campbell's soup can calling *someone want this grease?*, the old heads playing spades at their table, and the strange part was that no one was unhappy, considering.

When I got closer, I saw that the girl was eating cornstarch from a box. White powdered her chin. My key was in the lock when I thought I'd better ask her inside to wait. Inside was half upside down. Odds and ends that hadn't been there that morning were at my feet: a couple dug up plants from somebody's garden, too many fistfuls of still-good relish packets, and a stroller—one of those ones they got for running the baby—sleeping a tall orange cone in it. I stepped around the mess and went in my room to change into dry clothes.

My mother—the one I call Excuse—will inch the socks off your sleeping feet and I knew at once something of mine was missing, but I felt I was better off not knowing what she took until I needed it since it was gone now and wouldn't be coming back, whatever it was. I put on button-fly Levi's, Converse and a red hoodie. Back in the living room, Maeya stood at the window.

"Where's *your* Mom?" I asked.

"Out." Maeya shrugged, unfazed.

She watched me as I gathered up my crabber's gloves and yellow waders and CD player and locked them in my trunk. "You don't go to school?" she asked.

"They put me out."

"You must be bad," she said, looking me over.

"The principal got robbed."

Her mouth went slack. "Stop playing."

"Psyche," I said. "They got me for eating pop tarts in the bathroom."

"That's it?"

"I'm tired of school anyway. They always on you to write something. Even after you do your answers. They'll even take your scratch paper."

I walked to the window to see what she was looking at. Outside there were workmen everywhere. Some dudes in hardhats were wrapping columns in something. There was a trailer marked D E M O L I T I O N. Further off, other men in masked space helmets held blow-torches over manhole covers. I'd no idea why. Even Animal Control was out there unloading cage traps from a van.

"Dag," I heard myself whisper. "They getting ready."

"They're sure in a hurry for something," she said.

"If they gonna get rid of us, they better do it before it gets hot."

"What's the difference?"

"It'll be whatever then, Crayola. People stay upset for nothing when it's hot."

"They're upset now."

"Upset crazy. Not upset bawling."

From seven, the concrete square below looked split by green spider legs of grass, all hairy and tall. We could see people clutching plastic bags or humping boxes. Every so often, people would stop and huddle, shaking their heads, hugging—might've even been crying—before stepping through that grass. They did not seem to be in a hurry, but kept on, going away. Some of these people I'd known my whole life and watching them gave me a funny feeling, like I was looking at something I might miss later.

"It must not have been as bad as everyone said," Maeya said.

"Or we got used to it."

She pressed her forehead against the window, looking down. "I've been waiting for them to say it's all been a big mistake, they didn't mean it and everyone can come back now."

"They're not gonna say that," I said.

"I know," she said. "But they should."

"You think so, huh?"

"I mean, don't they feel bad putting people out?" She turned back to me.

I stepped away, rubbing the cold out of an elbow acting like it thought it was still outside. "You don't ask the hamster spinning the wheel when he's had enough."

She squinted at me, lost. She had a round face and little porcelain saucers for eyes. They were the kind of gentle eyes a little girl is supposed to have.

I stretched out on the couch. I hadn't realized how tired I was.

That Rent-A-Center left-behind was just right. I reached under the couch and grabbed two comic books—one Fantastic Four, one Hulk. I felt good, happy even. People had a lot to say about me and my comic books. Excuse said I was too old for them, but I'd never seen her read *anything*. Other people said comics ain't real, but what I need real for? I had plenty of that right outside my door. Basically, people'll tell you anything, if you let them. I closed my eyes. The heel and pitch of the boat were still under me.

Even now, with a whole bunch of cyclone fencing around the nothing where our home used to be, people still feel sad the way Maeya felt sad then, tattooing *FHP Forever* on their arms or necks. That was funny to me—inking up your body with a place that doesn't even exist anymore. I guess they thought it'll make 'em feel a little less empty for the people that used to be there. My Nana called it nostalgia, like worrying about the Colts all these years later.

All of us—me, Excuse, Maeya—picked up and dragged ourselves to my Nana's on the west side, which is where all this mess started. By then Maeya had been staying with us during those last weeks before they blasted our building to the ground. Nana said she'd get custody of Maeya when someone started asking, but no one ever did.

Nana was sixty-three, worked for Social Security, and drank a prune-gin cocktail before taking out her teeth each night. At night the teeth slept grinning, ready to talk, in the water glass on Nana's bathroom sink. I'd stayed with Nana before—once when I missed a lot of kindergarten and the school sent the police and declared Excuse unfit. *Duh*. Once when I was eight and Excuse had me steal razors from Safeway and they caught me. Once a couple years ago after this Mexican maid at the Quality Inn let me hold that room with a Jacuzzi for nothing until I got found out. Bunch of other reasons I can't remember right now. Nana was Excuse's mother, but they weren't nothing alike. Nana's is where you went when you wanted someone to ask what you wanna be when you grow up. She was never one of those pinch-your-cheek grandmas, but she looked after me and took pride in her house, hanging the windows with beige lace, feather-dusting the good china, which never came out the cabinet anyway, vacuuming when there was nothing to vacuum. She could cook too. Pans of lasagna, baked macaroni and cheese, big gravied roasts she served on egg noodles. And you didn't have to play sick to get any of it.

About Excuse, Nana'd say *she uses the toilet on us just like spelling her name.* I think Nana wanted to be free of her daughter and I was the thing that stopped her. Nana never said this. It's what I thought was all.

No one believed Excuse's promises about getting herself together once we were on the west side 'cause she never had herself together over east. That first week, though, we were counting our own shadows 'cause Excuse had trouble running her little outside scams and she'd steal the soap bar out the shower to try to sell it.

It might've been the second or third night after we got to Nana's. We sat around, trying to act normal. Maeya was messing with a rainbow hula hoop Nana had brought home. Nana sat in her recliner, working the crossword. Excuse was smoking at the window and I could see Nana clocking her over the top of the opened newspaper. There was a sour-sounding piano in the living room that Nana claimed Excuse could play once, but I'd never believed it.

I stepped over to the piano. "Play me a song, Ma."

Excuse acted like she hadn't heard me.

"You can't play, can you?"

She blew smoke out the window.

"Nana, she can't play," I said.

"She loved that piano. She was the only one that could play," Nana said, "Scott Joplin, Fats Waller, even some Bartok."

I pressed down a handful of keys. It jangled like an old toy. "You got jokes, Nana."

"I wish I did," Nana said, working the crossword.

I opened the bench lid and looked at the thin books of sheet music, the old scribbled notes on some pages. "I don't care what Nana says. I don't think you can play," I said.

"And you can stop, Franklin, okay? I got enough to forget without you bringing shit up, but there you go asking about a piano." She twisted her cigarette into the brick sill outside and left it there.

I closed the seat lid again.

"It was a long time ago," Excuse said, getting up. "I played then. I don't now. What you wanna kick a can? I can't change nothing what happened. You ain't Chopin yourself."

She walked into the hall and was out there with her hands on her lower back for a minute trying to get herself together when she called me over, away from Nana and Maeya. We stared at each other, neither of us speaking. Then she said, "I'ma need something."

I kept quiet.

She said softly, "You know it's different over here. I don't know these people like that."

"What you expect—a marching band?" I said. "They out there, jamming."

"I'm in the hole with that little crew already. I need help. I'm going sick."

"I ain't got no money," I lied.

She searched my face, playing back the words in her ear. Then she said, "Can you ask your man Alvin to front you something?"

I let my gaze rest on Excuse's face. It wasn't a pretty face anymore: a bony jaw, a droopy lower lip, two scheming dusty eyes. She could be charming or ugly, depending. This was charming.

"Can you do that for me, Franklin?" she said.

"I ain't seen him."

"I'm quite sure he's on his little strip or whatever."

I cut a quick glance over at Nana. She was still eased back in her recliner, snapping her newspaper, making little humming sounds. "Then ask him yourself," I said.

"He don't know me from Ronald Reagan." This was a favorite phrase of hers, even when it wasn't true.

I'd known Alvin from all those times at Nana's. We'd clicked since the fourth grade. Six months might pass without seeing him, then next time, there he was, a bouncy little guy with a smile so full of golds it stayed lit in there. We battled about anything—who could burp loudest, who had the nicest crossover, who choked on that first Newport and who didn't, who could sweet talk a seven out the dice, who went harder, east side or west. I kept a box cutter up in the cupboard above the fridge and now I reached up and slipped it in my pocket. When my coat went on, Nana plucked off her glasses, fed up. At the door I told Excuse, "Stay here."

Nana's was an old street, sunken in its middle like the power lines above, dip-strung, party-ribboned end to end, one block after the next. I walked up to the carry-out with the sign that said Mel's but everyone called Up Top. Two boys, almost yellow under the street lights, were posted up outside the store. I didn't recognize them and I had to think if I really wanted to ask these corner boys anything. I stepped in front of one. "You seen Alvin?"

The boy was blowing into his hands. A Bin Laden coat swallowed him. On his head, a blue bandana. His eyes were empty. "You gonna make his money right?"

"I don't know nothing about that," I said.

He sized me up, sucked his teeth. "Yeah, you look like short money."

I took him for one of those clowns that'll come at you sideways just to impress his friends. In my pocket I felt for the switch on the box cutter. I started to say, "Tell him"—

"You can't read?"

He undid his bandana and wrapped it again, knotting it off in the back. "Yo illiterate," the boy laughed, doubling over.

I didn't move. Then I saw the white letters behind and above him eating into the red brick: RIP Alvin. Inside me something skipped and dropped away. I backed up slowly, then turned and started up the empty street. A necklace of unlit doorways, boxy and empty, stretched up the block. Then I thought of his sister. I had not seen her for a long time, but remembered Alvin saying she'd gone to Philly for college, and I knew she must be tore up, wherever she was. Later, I'd find out some of what had happened—he'd messed up somebody's money, wouldn't get low when most would've—but none of it mattered. Alvin had always wanted to be hard. Now he was gone, and it didn't get any harder than that.

Back at the house, Excuse was sitting outside on the steps, arms clasped over her knees, rocking. When she saw me, she popped up. "What you got?"

"Nothing." I brushed past, opened the door and stepped into the house.

"Nothing?" She was on my hip. "What you mean?"

"Alvin ain't there."

"What about them others down there—you tell 'em you cool wit him?"

"Alvin. Ain't. There," I whispered, biting off each word.

"Oh shit," she said, catching something final and done in my voice.

"Yeah," I said. "Tish ho."

"He wasn't no older than you," she said.

I put my coat on a hanger in the closet. Behind me I heard Excuse say to no one in particular, "It's rough out here."

I paused in the hollow of that closet. When I turned around, she was squared up with me and that lemme-hold-a-dollar hunger was back in her eyes.

"Let me have that little radio of yours," she said. "I'll pay you for it after."

"You can't have my CD player," I said, trying to brush her off.

"Then I'll just take Maeya down the store."

I laughed. "Yeah, okay."

"I'll have her back in five minutes."

"Or five days."

"You just being stingy now."

I turned and hooked her elbow. "Ain't I always?"

She wrenched free, started clawing her neck, screeching *Am I gonna be alright? Am I gonna be alright? Am I gonna be alright?* Spit, like sparks, flew from her lips. I saw Maeya coloring with markers, spying the whole thing. I saw Nana, still resting in her recliner, set down the newspaper. Then I did the thing I swore I wouldn't: I gave

Excuse twenty dollars from my check I cashed the day before. The whole time I was thinking Barnacle Bob might as well be paying me in salt-water shivers for all this. I just wanted her out of the house. She snatched the money and was gone.

I stepped outside and watched her cut across the street and disappear around the corner. A sharp wind shaved the block of row houses. There'd be times she wouldn't come back for days. I used to worry she might be gone for good, but I learned that Excuse always made it home. Might forget her own birthday but she knew how to find home.

I closed the door. The house felt suddenly quiet. I let myself tip back, shoulders resting against the wall. Nana had been sitting on her purse. Now she stood, dug in her wallet, pulled out a twenty, walked it over and squeezed it into my hand.

I could tell you how awful it was having a mother who's a fiend, but I've accepted it. I could tell you it's just one side of her, but it's not. I could tell you that she wouldn't do anything for five dollars, but she would. I could tell you that when I was little and I needed her like I don't now, she loved me enough to stop, but she hadn't. I could tell you that I never saw this happening to Alvin, but I guess I had. I could tell you that when Excuse started running the streets over here, doing her little shiesty dirt, that the dude she hooked up with wasn't all bad, but Amon was.

Excuse introduced me to Amon this way. I was folding a bundle of clean laundry Nana had left on the couch. They came in together. Over her shoulder, Excuse said, "This a friend of mine" and breezed past, clattering down the hall, into the bathroom where she shut the door. Excuse wore a lot of noisy hoop bracelets, which she thought made her look legit.

I turned to face him. He was big and missing one eye. This surprised me, but I concentrated on keeping my gaze level, pretending he had two good eyes and one wasn't all milky with little smeary folds and creases that looked like they might be hissing.

I said, "Who are you?"

"The one and only, Amon." It sounded like an apology.

"Why is it the one and only?"

"Why is *what*?"

"Why is it the one and only?" I asked again

He stepped into the kitchen, real smooth, like it was his house and always had been and he was helping himself to whatever. He came right out, holding a can of peaches that had been in the cupboard, and talking again. "How you gonna ask me a question like that?" he said.

I shrugged and continued separating clothes. I saw then that Nana had bought Maeya a lot of new clothes: Hollister Jeans, a yellow American Eagle sweatshirt, socks with moons on them.

"Well, how many people you ever been around named Amon?" he asked.

"No one, I guess."

"Now, if you knew that you'd never known anyone named Amon then why'd you ask the question?" He had a goofy way of talking, like his mouth was a gurgling drain, *glub glub glub*.

"Just something I said, I guess."

He stepped a few steps closer and a sweet smell of talc came with him. "You went and fucked up the origin, is what you did."

I felt my back stiffen. I said, "I just never heard a name like that before."

"It was my people's inspiration. My people are from Togo."

You never knew who Excuse might bring in. In general, she was the type of person that could get you hurt—put you in the middle of something you got nothing to do with. But this jack-ass was wild-looking. Everything on Amon was too big. His hands were too big, his belly was too big, and his red, flappy-eared, peanut head was too big. He had to cock his face to get any seeing out of his one good eye.

"You know about Togo?"

"No."

"Then speak up, boy. Don't sit there like you Mr. *National Geographic*."

My feet shifted a little.

He made a couple clucking sounds. "Think you slick. Your Mom must notta raised you right."

"What's she got to do with it?"

"That ain't some soup du jour. That's your mother."

"And I raised myself," I said.

"Togo's in Africa," he went on, cutting me off. "It was German. A colony of it. That's what they called it anyway. A *colony*. Make it sound more proper for when the tea leaves and spices ain't yours no more 'cause the laws they made said so." Now he began to raise his voice. "Yes, indeedy. You looking at a hybrid. Dues paid. For keeps. Sweetened by the taker and the tooken."

I was quiet, but in my head I was thinking, wasn't they German in that movie they showed at school, the one where the dude saved the Jews? And this jack-ass didn't look nothing like them.

I heard the top pop on that little can of peaches and looked up. He sipped the syrup first, keeping the rim close to his lips, and lasering that one eye into me. "I expect you one of those ain't no use explaining nothing to, ain't you?" he said, smacking those peaches.

We watched each other, waiting. When I did not answer, he flicked his face at me, and spoke through his teeth, "Thought not."

A few days later, I came home from work and when I glanced out the window I saw Maeya standing in the alley. I clanged down the back metal steps. She was holding a shoebox. She stood beside some old tires and a torn mattress with popping springs. "What're you doing?" I asked.

"Looking for a butterfly," Maeya said.

I breathed in. Spoiled milk soured the air. Junk was everywhere.

"It was from school. I had it in here." She offered me the shoebox. Dime-sized holes had been cut on top. "Amon threw the whole thing out," she said, pointing up to the window.

"Why'd he do that?"

"Said we don't need no bugs in the house," she said.

I stood there, mad.

"It was red and black," she said.

I followed her as she picked her way deeper into the alley, stepping over a fan and plastic milk crate, looking behind a box spring. Then she stopped, turned around, straining to see between the spaces in all that junk. Her hands flapped out from her side and fell back.

"C'mon now," I said, "let's go in the house."

We started towards the mouth of the alley. "My teacher told us they don't taste good to birds," she said, hopefully.

Inside, Maeya sat down on the living room couch and I put on Oprah. I checked the rooms for Amon; he was gone. I dropped onto a cushion beside Maeya. Oprah was talking to dieters. These people had been on some crazy diets. They'd show a before picture of some humongous man and then some skinny dude would walk out and everyone would clap.

"Do you think my mother hates me?" Maeya asked.

"No," I said. "She loves you."

"She hasn't come looking for me, in case you hadn't noticed."

"She knows you're safe."

"She knows where I am?"

"Yes."

"Did she ask you to take me?"

"When you were staying with us all those nights and she didn't say nothing—that was like her asking."

Maeya seemed to think hard about this. "That's when my Mom knew I was across the hall. Now we're over west."

"You don't like Nana's cooking?"

"No, I do."

"Doesn't Nana keep your hair done?"

"Yes, she does."

"You'd rather be with your Mom somewhere?"

"Not when she's dropping me at different people's houses all the time. Her little while never is."

I didn't say anything. On the television Oprah was cheesing for some man that had lost a hundred and thirty-seven pounds. "He did good," Maeya said.

"Listen," I said, "did you know that your Mom and mine are just alike?"

She squinted at me. "Sort of."

"Oh, yeah. They have a lot in common."

"Like what?"

"Well, for one thing, they're both un-Moms."

"What's an un-Mom?" she asked.

"It's a Mom that can't be a Mom right now but might be a Mom again later."

"Oh," she said.

We were silent.

"You have a un-Mom?" she asked.

"Biggest in town."

"For how long?"

"Pretty much always, might as well say."

"Aren't you mad?"

"Used to be."

"*Used to be?*"

"I decided I can live with a Mom that ain't a Mom."

"Well, I'm mad," Maeya said.

"You gotta right."

She was quiet.

"It lasts long?" she asked.

I didn't have the heart to say long enough to make waiting for a normal life pointless, which is what I was thinking, so I just said, "Sometimes."

She was biting her lower lip. Oprah was talking about miracle berries and bloating.

"You know I used to fight for my mother?" The memory seemed sad and funny now and I felt a grunting snort come up. "Other kids would get to talking about her, calling her monkey fiend, or Junkie Diane, or whatever and I'd take up for her. I'd be out there, seven years old, scrapping in the street 'cause someone said she smelled like dukey, which she probably did."

Maeya was quiet.

"I was never too young for anything. That's just how she carried it," I said. "I wish somebody woulda pulled me up back then and told me: this woman's not changing for nothing."

"Who would've known that?"

"No one, I guess." I brushed some dirt off my tennis and felt a sigh go out of me. "It's just something you tell yourself in your head."

We were quiet for a time.

Then Maeya asked, "How'd my mother look when you told her I was gonna come stay with you and Nana?"

"What d'you mean?"

"You know, did she have her regular game face on and everything?"

"Oh, that," I said. "No, not at all. She got real sad."

"Is that all?"

"You could tell, it just hurt her real bad. But she was glad too 'cause she knows Nana keeps a good home."

Maeya was quiet. The truth is I admired the little girl. At her age, I was already half-sprung. This child hardly frowned. Might be scared of Freddy Kruger, but she was ready for whatever the world put on her.

I looked at her. "You alright?"

She nodded.

I held out my fist. "FHP."

I waited.

Then she balled her little fist, extended it and we tapped knuckles. "FHP," she said.

Everything looked different from the water. In the harbor the boats were shiny with linseed or resin, bobbing in their slips, and the light on the water was creased and flinty and the skyscrapers behind were struck glassy with sunlight and the city looked like a postcard a tourist might buy, and not at all like a place where anything could happen. Then as the boat moved further out, drawing a tail of foamy wake, the harbor spread out and the picture held your whole view and it could seem like a place you might leave one day, if you knew how, or someone showed you.

Barnacle Bob called himself an old salt and I guess that's how he talked too. When we got to the crab pots, he'd shift down to the little trolling motor and come out of his little pilot-house and start plucking my nerves with his sing-songy directions, *Swing to now. Drop the brailer. Hook that float. Now heave.* He would say the same thing three, five, seven times. His voice would be low and steady, like something he learned in church, and after a while it would seem like his little sayings were keeping time with the water.

There were heavy seeping chains and small anchors and big crab pots. These I hoisted up, hand over hand. Every time I dropped a pot or pulled up another coil of chains, Barnacle Bob was right there with *Swing to now.* And it was kind of funny, but his talk did sort of help you bring the weight up and over the edge and on to the deck.

And Barnacle Bob knew that bay like I knew the streets. He'd look at the moon and tell you about the tide, listen to the water against the hull and tell you about the wind, tell you what trap was coming from which side way before you got your first glimpse of blue marker buoy, tell you where the grasses grew underwater from how the water sat, smell the wind and guess just where the northerlies would've dried out the marshes. He probably could've done it all stone blind. He didn't fool with charts or sounding devices or tide tables. He knew the shoals and where the channels played out because he'd always known them. And if anyone ever cut his traps, Barnacle Bob was ready for blood.

Sometimes the pots were more or less empty, or had only a few eels, which we'd use for bait, and Barnacle Bob would get heated and start talking down the winter dredgers or the algae that had no business growing in the water or the government trying to keep him on the beach. But he didn't stay mad. It was like Barnacle Bob hadn't made up his mind about everything yet, which probably explained why he'd hired me to begin with, 'cause I know I looked like a roughneck bopping through his door that first time.

If the pots were empty, we'd drive out Route 1 to buy "Barnacle's Catch" from the freezers at Sysco. Along the way, he'd be playing Hank Garland or Chet Atkins in his truck and it was as if those empty pots out on the water had been someone else's. With his moon face and yellow beard and the sling shots going half up his back, Barnacle Bob was like something out of one of my comic books, except he never really wanted to get even with anybody.

One day we were far out and when I snagged the last float for the last pot and pulled it in, it was empty like the others before it. It had been another bad day, the fourth in a row. I reset the bait box with fresh chicken necks, raised it to the edge, and listened for Barnacle Bob's *swing to now* as I set the pot in the water and paid out the line. Then Barnacle Bob did something unusual. He cut the engine and let the boat drift. He was quiet and didn't seem in the mood for talking. I sat down on the rusty water breaker and zipped up my fleece hoodie. Using my clenched teeth, I tightened my gloves and then crossed my arms against the cold. The bay was empty in every direction. There was hardly a current. I felt that something might be wrong, like Barnacle Bob was hurting somehow and it made me feel bad for ever wishing his pots come up light.

Barnacle Bob stood looking out beyond the stern. In the open water, drifting, time felt slowed.

"The sky looks funny, sitting on the water like that," I said.

He did not answer for a time. "I suppose it does."

"What's out there?" I asked.

"A few shore towns gone so broke they're more mud hens than people," he said, still without turning around.

"What if you keep going?"

"You'll be in the Atlantic."

"And then, after that?"

"The rest of the world."

The weather was turning. The sky was papier-mached in gray, a thousand shades of gray. It would be dead winter soon and the crabs would dig in and go in their holes and Barnacle Bob would pack it in 'til spring because he didn't believe in dredging. For a time, we drifted, listening to the bay slapping softly against the quarters. Then I said, "It's a long ways from here?"

He had turned back to me. "What's that?"

"The rest of the world."

Amon came to the back door, pounding. Excuse started for it, but I headed her off. "Don't bring him in here again," I said.

"What you getting ready for tea and crumpets?"

Nana had been watching *Jeopardy*, but now she was up, crossing the room towards us. I felt like Nana was aging before our eyes. She looked a hundred and three.

"I don't like him," I said.

"Sit your tail down," Excuse said. "He ain't no harm to nobody."

"No more than you," Nana said. "And that's enough for anybody."

"Whatever," Excuse hissed.

He pounded the door again. Nana moved forward and slid back the dead bolt and pulled the knob. Stone-faced, Amon filled the doorway, one arm on the jamb.

"You'll have to take your good times outside, sir," Nana said. "There are children in this house." The door clicked shut again.

On the way out, Excuse wheeled on me. "That's the problem with you: you always think you better than somebody."

Sometimes I sang Maeya to sleep with one of those girl-power songs by Alessia Cara or India Arie. I can sing a little bit, but only Maeya would know it. This night I didn't feel like singing so I was searching for a good radio station. I'd gotten tired of 92 Q playing the same songs.

She said, "You're like my father, Franklin."

"I'm not your father, Maeya."

"I think so."

"Sixteen's not old enough to be a father."

"Yes, it is."

"Not yours."

"Then why do you hold my hand when we get on the bus?"

"So you don't fall and bust your ass and everyone laugh at you."

"Isn't that like a father?"

"No."

"I think it is."

"Look, Maeya, your father's in Jessup. You know that."

"So?"

"So quit geeking."

"But I don't even talk to him."

"That's still your father," I said.

"Not to me."

"And he probably gave you those good smarts," I said, "least you could do is act like you use 'em."

We were quiet while I fiddled with the radio dial. Bits of songs flew by.

"Amon says he knew my father."

"That fool'll say anything. He never knew your father."

"He said you act like you're grown when you're not."

I thought about how kids my age always think they're grown and want to tell anyone who'll listen. But I didn't think I was grown. Instead, I thought about getting older and what my life would be like then. But I didn't say any of this to Maeya. I said, "He could be two hundred, but that don't make him grown."

"He said he's gonna teach me to kiss, since I'm gonna be a woman soon."

I cut the radio off. "*What?*"

"*Someone's gotta show you how a woman be,*" she put her hands on her hips and puffed out her chest, imitating the *glub-glub-glub* of Amon's voice. "*A woman's gotta know how to enjoy herself.*"

I got up, my shirtfront in my teeth, cursing. Then I threw open a window and spat. I asked Maeya a bunch of other questions, but she didn't say much more and I just got madder anyway.

Afterwards she said, "You shouldn't cuss."

"Even that bastard knows better than talking like that to you."

"I don't pay Amon no mind."

I said, "You stick by me or Nana. Okay?"

She was quiet.

I took her hands in mine. "Tell me you heard me."

"I did," she said.

"You promise now?"

She nodded.

My bed had been in the very small room Nana always called a sewing room. Now I dragged my little mattress down the hall and into Maeya's bedroom. I plumped the pillows and arranged the bedding on the floor where I slept for a time after this. She watched me, her face still with worry. I hadn't meant to scare her.

"Look," I said, "Amon ain't right. Even when he does something nice—like gives you a whole box of Krispy Kremes, all your own—he's really just plotting on something else."

She said, "His eye—that ugly one—it looks funny."

"Somebody told him no."

The next day Amon came in from the back. I was in the kitchen, making a bologna and Miracle Whip sandwich.

"You can't be in here no more."

"Say who?"

"This not your house."

He looked at me, surprised. "What you tipsy?"

"Wouldn't matter if I was," I said.

"Your Mama's already gave it her blessings," he said, like that settled it.

"That ain't even how she talks," I said. "She ain't church." I placed my sandwich back on the plate and set it on the counter. "So you can bounce."

"Oh, you big time now," he said. "You decided."

"Maeya doesn't need you anywhere near her. None of us do."

Suspicion twisted his face. "You must be planning on keeping her to yourself." He opened the refrigerator door, closed it and swung back to me, getting louder. "'Cause you sure enough not running, what, an orphanage in here?"

"I'll take that key." My voice had gone tight.

When he moved closer, you could feel his size in the floor. "Nine ain't what it used to be. Girls grow up fast nowadays." And then he laughed, throat like a train tunnel.

"You make me sick," I said.

I never felt him hit me. First, I was standing; then laid out. Darkness pooled around me and the smell of bologna became electric, crackling and sputtering behind my eyes. I lay there, trying for breath. I heard him changing TV stations. Then I remembered the weight of his shoulder rolling towards me before the fist shot out. High in the chest is where he'd hit me.

When I got to my elbows, he came over and put a heel on my throat, flattening me. "I seen so much I gave one of these sum bitches back." And he pointed to the empty socket in his face. "You lucky I left you something to chew your food wit."

I got to my feet and started for the bathroom. I was up and walking, but I was shaky. At the sink I steadied myself before the mirror.

My wind felt small; it made a little rattle. Slowly, I cranked my head, right, then left, until my breathing got easier. I had not expected a warning and there had been none. I opened the medicine chest; the reflection of my eyes swung past. There was a box of Band Aids and some mouthwash. I didn't need Band Aids or mouthwash.

I headed down to the corner where Alvin used to be. I thought of asking one of them that took his place to kill Amon but didn't. Then I went looking for Maeya.

The next day I didn't go to work. Barnacle Bob would have to do it without me. I did hope the crabs were running for him, but I wanted to be in the house when Maeya came in from school, which I was.

The sun was gone from the sky. It was getting to be time for dinner. I'd gotten paid the day before, so I had some money. Maeya was eating cornstarch from the box, a habit I hadn't been able to break her from. She looked bored, flicking jacks around her lap on the carpet.

"You keep eating that, you gonna turn into a ghost," I said. "Watch."

"I wanna bake a cake," she said.

I was getting mad. "Fix your face. You look a mess."

"What's wrong with you?" she asked.

"It's not food."

"You're acting funny." She sounded insulted. "And bossy."

"Yeah, well, maybe I got things on my mind."

She closed up the box and brushed off her mouth and cheeks. "Anybody can bake a cake," she said. "Just follow the recipe."

We were quiet.

"We don't have no eggs, anyway," I said. "I'm quite sure that recipe says eggs. I know that much."

"Chinese people deliver," she said.

"If you think I'm calling that Chinese man and asking him for two eggs."

"Why not?" she said. "I don't mind calling."

I forced out a long breath. Maeya could argue if four quarters made a dollar when she wanted to. "You a nuisance," I sighed, giving in.

We walked down to the corner store and bought all the ingredients in the recipe. By the time we got back and got started, Nana was home. Later, after Meaya's yellow sheet cake had cooled and she was icing the top and Nana dozed in her chair and the whole house smelled cake-sweet, I let myself fall into that butterscotched air where you could tell yourself all the trouble coming down wasn't about to get worse.

I asked some dudes around the way about Amon. He'd done a lot of cruddy things. Stolen his uncle's methadone so he could sell him real dope. Called the fire department once faking concussion for an Advil. Ran in the Arabber's pockets and, when all he got was a peach pit and someone laughed, Amon killed the dude's sable-back horse right there; after that, was like a fruit drought hit the whole neighborhood. Always ready to mix in. Always wants a Newport but never has one for anybody else.

If I called the police on Amon, they'd come in here and take Maeya away, put her in some crazy foster home or group home or in DSS. Might even try to put me somewhere.

I thought of tricking Amon into coming out on the boat—

telling him we can rob Barnacle Bob—then knocking Amon's big ass in the water. I doubted he could swim and no one would miss him. But I didn't think Barnacle Bob would appreciate me using his boat like that.

I wished so hard that something would happen to Amon, but nothing did. Life was like that. Amon could rob and steal and scheme and get over and nothing hardly happened to him. But Alvin tries to sell a few pills for back-to-school clothes, and he gets got.

A day later I went down the back steps to where Amon always came in. I slipped into the alley, beside the steps.

I turned a metal trashcan upside down, pulled it into a sliver of darkness, away from the streetlight and sat. Patience filled me. I'd wait 'til next spring if it took that. I felt the grapple in my hand. It was iron, heavy, and had three small hooks. I did worry that I didn't have it in me to crack his skull, or that I wouldn't hit him hard enough and then he'd just burn me up with the revolver he kept in his dip. So many dudes say, *You can't be scared. Live by, die by. Real knows real.* But when they're on that sidewalk leaking out of themselves, they're scared. Crying for their Mama-God-ambulance, they're scared.

Hours passed and the sun went down and I set myself against these worries. There was an old head of cabbage under the steps and the rats ate from it, taking their time. And I got to wondering about the things I always wonder about: the stars of course and what's so great about this country that everyone wants to come here for anyway, and Nana's teeth in that water glass at night and what Alvin saw when that cap went in his nose—maybe it just feels like clicking off the TV, that sucking sound and everything shrink-popping black. And the rats came out deep, scurrying here and there and I could hear a TV from someone's house. It was a re-run of *Martin*.

Then I heard him, walking that shuffling walk, mumbling, re-living a bad turn he owed somebody. My ears pricked up. My breath dropped away. I bent my knees and clenched back the grapple with my moisty grip. I could feel blood thumping my head. He got so close I smelled that sweet powdery talc he wore and I saw his face emerging from a curtain of cigarette smoke and at the last moment he turned that one good eye toward me and I swear I heard Barnacle Bob in my head.

"Swing to! Swing to! *Swing to now!*"

He took the Jones Falls Expressway, the river hurtling past. In the city, Seth drifted along old streets freckled in brick and grooved with left-behind streetcar rails going nowhere. He passed under a stone railroad trestle smoldering in red and yellow graffiti. He liked that he was alone. He could look at what he wanted, steer his father's Navigator wherever, and never explain himself to anyone.

He pulled to a curb and parked. Clean-shaven, solid through shoulders draped in dark leather, he carried himself loosely, checking out these blocks, pretending this world—its seeping manholes and live chickens crated outside the Chinese buffet, pitched sidewalks and tattered billboards—was his and always had been.

At a park with plank benches and a dry fountain, he sat. The brick faces of the row homes—soot-misted, under steep slate roofs—looked like they'd been there a long time and he wondered what life was like back then. He watched the pigeons; he watched the people. Some looked like they had nowhere to go; others wore hard faces.

Seth tried hardening his own features. He thought of the baseball team he'd quit last season. His teammates had brought out a cocky posturing in each other and in him. But it had always just been talk—empty or speculative. Nothing ever happened.

It was on one of these days that he met her. He saw her from half a block away and understood she was beautiful even before he could really make out her features. The row house steps she sat on let down near the Navigator. She wore silver hoop earrings and a shiny pink athletic suit, the pants matching the zip-up top. Her hair was pulled back and streaked with gold. She was chewing gum, and there was something sneering and pouty in the way her mouth worked it.

"You lost?" she asked.

He nodded towards the car. "Just getting my car."

"You don't go to school?"

"Sometimes."

"What reason you got for not going?"

He shrugged.

"You have to have a *reason*."

"It's boring."

"Not like that. A real reason."

"Like what?"

"Problems, you know. Like your mama's a club girl and it's got you all messed up. Something like that. "

"My mother?" His eyebrows lifted in surprise. "She goes to parties. But only 'cause she feels obligated."

"Okay, then your dad brings women in the house, threatens to whip your ass if you tell?"

"My dad wouldn't hit me," Seth said. "Plus, he's not really home enough for all that."

"Maybe you got high lead?"

"Which is what?"

"Lead poisoning."

"How would I know if I have that?"

"You'd be slow."

Seth paused to consider this.

"My cousin did. He was real off. Used to zap out on the mailman for waking him up," she said. "He's locked up now. No one cares if you got lead once you're grown."

Seth was silent.

"Anyway," she chomped her gum dismissively. "They would've told you by now."

The sun was bright and you could smell a chill in the air, riding the breezes.

"How do you know I don't go to school, anyway?" Seth asked.

"I seen you."

"Oh yeah?"

"Don't get your head swolled, sweetie. It ain't like you ain't sticking out."

She sat with her elbows on her knees, squinting in the sun. Seth sunk his hands into the pockets of his black jeans and toed a bit of sidewalk grit. He looked at the car. "You wanna go for a ride?"

"I don't know you like that."

He aimed the key fob, and the locks on the Navigator chirped open. "Tomorrow maybe?"

She was sizing him up, wary, then looked away. "I probably don't even see you again."

Seth's mother had started her career as a nurse, and now ran a company in Singapore that sold IV food to hospitals all over Asia. His father was an insurance executive. This week he was in Toronto. Home Sunday. Then away again. They had amassed a small fortune. Seth figured they could ease up, work less, if they wanted.

The next morning, when Seth should have been in trigonometry, he sat at the kitchen table, eating Cheerios in cold milk and reading the *Baltimore Sun*. Seth read about famine in Sudan and disease in the Congo and war in Iraq or Afghanistan. On a low shelf with the cookbooks a big atlas was kept. The maps folded out, peach and marine, and dragging a finger over the broken countries he'd read about, Seth thought about how he'd never been hungry or war-torn or sick. He looked at his forearm, the muscles ropy and bunched from visits to the gym. He was strong, he knew that, and until recently his grades had been good. Still, he couldn't think of one thing he'd ever done that had called for any guts.

He didn't think he could explain this feeling to anyone or that anyone would understand. But he was eighteen now, and he felt he needed to do something to alter the course of his life.

The recruiter's office was in a strip mall beside a PetSmart. Inside it felt staged and ephemeral, like tomorrow it might be a Jackson Hewitt or a Dollar Store. The walls were draped with American flags and plastic-framed posters of sailors triumphing at the pitch of some extreme physical trial.

In his service khakis, the recruiter himself looked lean and authoritative. They sat at a table with brochures set upright in clear pocket stands. "Thought about college?" the recruiter asked, feeling him out.

"I've applied," Seth said. "People think you're lost if you don't."

"Maybe you'd rather stay home, take a job for a year. Nothing wrong with it."

"I wouldn't," Seth said.

"You wouldn't what?"

"I don't want to stay home."

"Have you talked it over with your parents?"

He paused. "No one knows I'm here."

The recruiter waited.

"They wouldn't like it," Seth said. "Probably not even a little."

"Why is that?"

"I'm sure they'd worry about me getting hurt."

"Not everyone in the Navy goes to Iraq. You might just as soon find yourself in Australia or Japan."

Seth glanced outside where a UPS truck idled at the curb. "It's just better they don't know about this."

The recruiter clasped his hands behind his head and offered a patient, confidential nod. "Well, it's your decision anyway, isn't it?"

He walked Seth over to a computer terminal and sat him down for the ASVAB test. After the machine tabulated Seth's scores, the recruiter pulled a chair right up to Seth's knee, crowding in.

"What do you wanna do, Seth? Because this might be your epiphany. Right here. Right now. No diploma required."

Seth wasn't sure joining the Navy wasn't a mistake—one with consequences he couldn't yet make out and might one day regret. He was still arranging it in his own head so it was going to be a while before he tried explaining it to anyone else.

The roads from his neighborhood wound past tall Tudor homes with crescent driveways. Winter would be over soon, and then the homes would be lost in the deepening green, but for now the trees were still bare. Blades of sunlight strobed off tree branches.

When he pulled in front of her house, she made a visor of her hands. "You must don't know what to do with yourself."

They drove around talking, but she hardly looked at him. Unsure where to go, Seth casually steered the SUV toward the Inner Harbor. Glassy boutiques and hotel lobbies rolled by.

"My Mom used to insist on bringing us down here for the tall ships," Seth said.

"You were one of those people waiting in line on TV?"

"Every year."

"People around my way don't come down here like that. Not for ships anyway."

"Why not?"

"I don't know. Some people just stay in their neighborhood. They'd probably say it's corny, basically."

Seth cracked the window, and crisp air slipped in.

"So how was it—the boats, I mean?" she asked.

"They were cool," Seth said. "You know, if you like that sort of thing."

She held out a pack of Wrigley's Doublemint. He unwrapped the foil and chewed the gum slowly. "It sounds stupid, but those ships did make my mother happy."

"She's not happy now?"

"She has everything she wants," Seth said. "I suppose she likes that."

"Doesn't she care you hook school?"

He tapped down the turn signal. "They don't know the difference."

He took Charles Street up the hill. Jeezy's "Soul Survivor" came on the radio. He turned it up and mouthed along.

"You're a trip," she said.

"Just 'cause I'm white doesn't mean I sit around watching NASCAR and listening to Toby Keith."

"It's not your fault," she said. "It's just you kinda look like it."

"Look like what?"

"Like you watch NASCAR or whatever."

His expression soured. "You're serious?"

"I mean it's okay if you do."

"You watch NASCAR."

"Yeah, alright," she said.

"Bet you can just sit there and watch 'em go round and round in circles all day. You probably even have your favorite drivers."

"Yeah, alright," she said again and smiled.

They eased around the Washington Monument, the cobblestoned rotary rattling the tires, and Seth pulled to the curb.

She glanced at the monument's column. "So big they gave him two: this one *and* the extra tall one in DC—what they call it? —an obelisk? Like a pyramid on a sky scraper, kinda."

"You like geometry or something?" Seth asked.

"I just used to memorize stuff. When I was little anyway," she said. "Crayon colors no one knew: periwinkle and ecru. The fastest bird. The lowest temperature. A squirrel's nest isn't a nest."

"What is it?"

"A drey," she said. "It's a drey. It looks like a nest. But they call it a drey."

"Teachers must love you."

"I hate school. They teach you the same thing every year: *quit, quiet, quite*. Three different words. *Duh?* I'm better off at the library, finding stuff out on my own. Anyway, I got my GED so I'm done." She palmed out a talk-to-the-hand sign, gloating.

She explained how she'd walked that brand new GED downtown and, all on her own, talked her way into a job in a company that washed windows in office buildings. "I had my button-down, blue work shirt—my own name stitched right here: Elegance." She was pointing below her collar and when she smiled, her teeth were so bright and neatly lined-up they seemed cut from polished stone. "You can live here your whole life and never go in any of those marble lobbies. It makes you feel legit, you know, like you're on your way to *something*. And my grandmother was happy, proud-like, too."

"And then one day"—she pressed together the heels of her palms—"It's hard to explain. Girls love a mirror, but the reflection staring back in all that lobby glass..." Her voice trailed off. "I just started to feel small."

"After a couple months you catch yourself wondering: does anyone even know I'm here? The important people carrying their Louis Vuittons? The Mexican women working beside you—Gomez and Gamez and Gallante— who only talk to each other and act like they wouldn't mind wiping down brass rails for another hundred years? The glass that was already shining and squeaking before you squeaked it some more? But it's not the kind of question you can ask anybody, is it?" She paused, as if still figuring it out herself. "I don't know what I expected. I know I was supposed to have been happy enough that I keep that job."

They were quiet.

"Anyway, I don't memorize stuff anymore," she said. "It was just a way to keep my mind busy when things got hectic."

Her attention settled back on the monument.

"If I make it to president, tell 'em don't build me one," she said.

"Why not?"

"They just sit there looking stupid. Tourists ride around on double-decker buses and say *what a pretty little city*. It ain't all it's cracked up to be." She paused. "Anyway, people should do their own thinking. Try to anyway. Don't put up a monument to tell me what to think."

Seth watched her.

"Name a hot sauce after me," she said. "Something people'll use. Don't make me into something I wasn't."

They were facing each other. In the sunlight her eyes softened and took on hazel.

"I'm not like the girls at your school," she said. "Am I?"

"How do you know?"

"I can just tell."

"We got pretty girls in the county too."

"That ain't what I meant."

"I know," he said. And she let him lean across the leather seats and kiss her. Above the rooftops, the sky was streaked yellow and gray and he felt his belly flutter.

When he got home that night, he could not sleep.

Then it was April and under a darkening sky they walked to a corner grocery. Her back was straight and her leggings were tight and sleek. Inside his Adidas, Seth's toes made fists.

The store was steamy with the smell of pretzels and cola. Dim shadows draped aisles stacked with canned Vienna sausages and ramen noodles and bins of fresh tomatoes and zucchini. Into their basket they placed barbeque Fritos, mint ice cream, fresh plums.

Outside a hard rain had come on. The air turned briny, blowing like a wind-whipped curtain. The streetlights blinked on and for a time they waited it out in the doorway, under an oval marquee, holding each other away from the curling mist. When Seth saw a taxi's gleaming box light floating up the street, he stepped from their shelter. He took his time, passing lazily over the stream guttering at the curb.

Beside the stopped taxi, Seth turned back to her. She saw him tip back, open-armed, open-mouthed, under the torrents of rain. She wagged her head at the goofy white boy she'd hooked up with, cupping a laugh with her hand. He was waiting now beside the open door. Zipping up her jacket collar, she readied herself, getting her own footing, shifting the bags from one arm to the other. Then she was off, her flying feet flashing lightly, barely letting up as she lowered herself into the open back seat. He slipped in behind her and pulled the door closed.

She straightened, breathing hard. "I'ma hurt you Seth Minor."

They had a few words with the driver who let the Mercury start rolling. Seth was shivering now, and she drew him into her arms. In the warmth of the cab, her perfume lifted, sweet and pretty. From the soggy brown bag, she took a plum and bit in. It was this taste of blue plum that gave Seth the contours of her mouth.

When they got back to her place, her grandmother stood beside the kitchen sink, arranging quartered potatoes and little onions around a roasting chicken. On the stove a pot of corn and lima beans stood ready to simmer. She turned and paid Seth the courtesy of a hello. The church van would be around any minute, she explained. She crimped a foil tent over the chicken and slid the pan into the oven. "Watch that roaster," she said to Elegance. "Don't let it dry out." She threw a dishrag at their feet, where the rainwater was puddling the linoleum, and shooed them out.

Upstairs they slithered out of their soaking clothes and Elegance toweled him off and they lay on their stomachs in her bed, listening to the rain tapping at the window. The sheets smelled sweetly of laundry soap and it felt good to be dry and under the warm blankets, beside each other. The radiator ticked. Seth traced a finger across the small of her back, spelling the letters of her name. Then he was inside her, moving with her.

In a robe and slippers, she picked up his jeans and turned out the pockets, putting his keys and wallet and phone on the window sill and then gathered up the rest of the heavy, wet clothes and, holding them away, went downstairs to the basement dryer. Seth heard her slippers slapping on the winding stairs. She had left the bedroom door open, and he wished now that she had not taken his wet clothes.

The good smells of the baking chicken and potatoes drifted upstairs, and Horace Silver played on a stereo from her uncle's room. The man, wiry and bearded, hardly left the house. Each month a check came for him from the VA. Sometimes he asked Elegance to buy him scratch-offs or milk of magnesia or batteries. Seth listened as the uncle broke in with the melody. His voice was so reedy and sweet Seth couldn't tell if it was the uncle singing or part of the recording.

After a while, Elegance returned and climbed back into bed. "You good?"

"Yeah," he said.

They were on their sides, facing each other.

"I never met anyone with a name like yours," Seth said. "It's unusual."

"My mother gave it to me," Elegance said. "It was a perfume. My mother named me after a perfume. Isn't that stupid?"

"It suits you," Seth said. "She must've known you were special."

"My mother's a joke. She's been getting herself together my whole life. Can't help herself. She's got no pride. That's what helpless is, right? When you got no pride?"

She sat up and leaned towards the window. The storm had broken and a seam of yellow light creased the sky. Down the hall, her uncle was keening a blues.

"We aren't even supposed to be together like this," she said.

"Why not?"

"That's what people think when they see us."

"Somebody said something?" Seth growled, pretending toughness.

"Just 'cause they don't say it doesn't mean they're not thinking it."

"I thought people are like M & M's. All the same on the inside."

"It's nice to think so. But they ain't following you around CVS."

From behind, he clasped his fingers around her belly and pulled her close. "Maybe they just like watching you walk."

She gave him a light, scolding tap on the knuckles. "I can't worry about them anyway," she said. "It's not my fault some people need to get a life."

He was kissing her neck. "Every day oughta be like this."

She cooed and between these murmurings she said, "You know, all the white boys I ever knew were either nerds or phony—just trying too hard to be down. You're regular."

"Just regular?"

"I mean you're cool. Normal," she said. "I like the way you are."

The days turned warmer. Occasionally, on hot afternoons, they sought out the cool air and the privacy of Seth's house. On this day, they'd been to Skateland and had gone back to Seth's house and now he was asleep beside her. For a while she lay against his warmth, listening to his breathing, which was warm and easy with sleep.

It was always a little hard for her to relax here. Inside his parents' house, she was reminded again of differences she'd sometimes forgotten. She worried that his parents could pop in unexpectedly. What would they think if they saw her? Would she say the right thing and would it sound proper enough? About his parents, Seth had offered reassurances, but maybe, for her sake, he had left some things out? Maybe there were things about his mother or father that he would not like to admit? Or things about them he had not seen himself? From the framed photos decorating the hallway—Seth and his father, in puffy, white parkas, ski goggles pushed high up their foreheads; his mother and father beside a deck railing above a green ocean—she pictured his parents having fussy manners and smiles so fake they might hurt themselves holding them up.

She sat up, looking around his bedroom: the posters of O's sluggers, the baseball caps he had collected from stadiums he'd visited over the years, a Fender bass guitar that he didn't play. Little souvenirs he'd picked up on vacations with his parents: a carved turtle from the Galapagos, nesting soldier dolls from St. Petersburg. She still marveled at the size of the room, the thick, bone-colored, wall-to-wall carpet catching sun from two skylights, a bathroom all his own, right off the bedroom.

She stood and looked down the hall to an upstairs den where brown leather chairs and an ottoman were arranged around a stone fireplace and the ceiling was coffered in dark wood. She crossed Seth's bedroom to the window, the carpet swallowing her steps. In the yard there was a gazebo and a little terraced pond and beyond that the edge of a golf course. It was so quiet. No voices on the sidewalk below; no sidewalks at all.

On a desk shelf, under a *World History* text, his school notebook sat. She flipped through the sections divided by plastic sleeves, stopping once to look at a chemistry syllabus, which confirmed something she'd already assumed: rich kids' school is different. She was going to jot a silly note, to tuck inside and surprise him with later. She also wondered if there might be notes from other girls in there.

When she unfolded the notification letter from the Navy, its blue-eagled seal coming into focus, it took the wind out of her. What emerged was a whispered question: "What?"

The world became suddenly small and brittle and in it she did everything slow. She put all the papers back, just as they had been. On the edge of the bed she sat down again and cupped her knees and measured out several full, even breaths; in, out; in, out; in, out. Beside her, he did not stir. She regarded his smooth cheek and close, thick hair, the muscle packed on his shoulder. She bent and gently laid her cheek on his chest and breathed in an odor that was by then sweetly familiar: some mix of aftershave, dried sweat and boy.

After a while, she swiveled and took his hands in hers and tugged him lightly awake. He came out of sleep fitfully, his face scrunched. Opening his eyes, he stretched drowsily, reached for her. She looked away, hiding her eyes. "What's wrong?" he asked. She stood. It was her stomach, she said, it didn't feel right. A hand to her belly, a wince. She wanted to go home. It was the truth.

The next day began for Seth as usual. He sat at the kitchen table and spooned cereal up to his mouth, looking over the newspaper. He read closely several articles about Iraq and one about Afghanistan. Seth did not linger on the pictures of a smoldering American tank, or another of a wounded marine being airlifted to Germany.

He went out to the garage and backed his father's SUV into the driveway. He unspooled the garden hose and filled a bucket and squeezed in Turtle Wax and started washing the hood first, working his way around. Afterwards, he drove to the gym and lifted weights and came back and showered and changed. He had started an online chess game with a man in Slovenia and he studied the Slovenian's response to his last move. It was late afternoon when Seth called and started for her place. On his way, she asked him to stop at T-Bones, a Creole diner, and pick up an order of gumbo.

He stood at the counter below the illuminated, orange menu. It smelled good, like garlic and hot oil and paprika. He ordered gumbo and catfish and hush puppies. Walking back to the car, he saw two boys start across the lot. They walked purposefully. One boy was lanky, moving with a bouncy gait and wearing a white John Elway throwback jersey. The other, squat and heavy-legged, lifted his face skyward, humming a ballad. He did not have the same blunted, determined expression as the taller boy, but kept pace nonetheless. Seth saw faded denim bunched at their ankles. He felt them closing and his stomach tightened.

It was a strip of radial tire—bobbing like a stubby, hidden tail— that the lanky boy pulled from his back waistband. The old rubber made a comic book *thwack* against Seth's head. He went down, the world dropping into an inky murk. This taller boy, repeating a line from a police drama he'd seen on television, called out, "man down!" which was answered in succession, "man down!" But Seth did not hear them. His wallet was turned upside down and raked out above his head. Bills of cash, credit cards, concert stubs, ids, little paper keepsakes fell on or beside Seth and the empty wallet fell too. He did not see the blue Nikes straddling his face, nor the hand that reached for the warm carry-out bag. Seth had the impression the sound itself had injured him. He wanted to say stop, there'd been some mistake, they had the wrong guy, but they were already gone and he did not speak. For a while he lay there. It was the stillness of everything that he became aware of first. He lifted his face. A cold roar phased in and out.

Seth was sitting up when a man with short, neat dreadlocks pulled up and walked over to him. He knelt beside Seth and pressed a clump of yellow Wendy's napkins to his bleeding head, told Seth to hold it there. The man began to sort of duck walk, collecting the scattered credit cards and money. He was eager to get them back into Seth's hands. "Hold 'em now," the man said, "these yours." He squeezed shut Seth's fingers for him. "Go on."

Still squatting, the man moved square in front of Seth. "Where's your car, son?"

Seth's eyes found the car across the lot, but he did not speak.

"Son?" the man asked.

Seth said, "It's there. It's that Navigator."

The man got him to his feet. He said, "You're alright." It wasn't a question, but a statement of assurance. When Seth didn't move, the man asked if he wanted an ambulance. Seth did not answer. A set of traffic lights at the corner seemed to thicken and bow. He was steadying Seth by the elbow, and he began guiding him towards the car. Seth could feel his neck stiffening. He reached back there and was surprised when his hand came back slick and runny. Seth checked his pockets, then realized everything was still in his hand.

He hadn't thought of his parents all day, but coming into the empty house, he felt their absence. They would be able to figure out how badly he'd been hurt, and they would know what to do. He thought hard to remember their schedules. One in Boston? Another Chicago? Or was that last week? Images of his parents in separate, sleek, hotel lounges unreeled before him. He made a mental note to check their itineraries on the kitchen calendar. For now he was alone in the house, and everything felt newly still. He looked at himself in the mirror. Dried blood caked his neck and the collar of his mint Polo pullover. A tremble, like a low electric current, ebbed through his hands. In the shower, he discovered a parcel of flapped skin on his scalp, roots and all. He used a washcloth and gently cleaned around it, watching the rust-colored water swirl past his feet.

He got out and, still hazy, looked at himself again in the mirror. His ears felt plugged. He considered driving himself to the hospital, then decided to wait. He changed into fresh clothes—a blue Champion pullover and gray Adidas sweat pants.

One hand on the banister, he took the stairs slowly down, as if he did not trust them. He stood at the landing and looked at the empty living room: the ox-eye window over the chenille sectional, two suede club chairs, the built-in, cubbied media center. All familiar, yet somehow not. He flicked on a bank of lights. Everything went bright. He knew he was alone, but he called out anyway: *Hello?*

He called her and got nothing, texted and received no reply. He cut on the TV, muted it, and thumbed in her numbers again. No answer. No answer. No answer. Keith Olbermann's big head, silently venting out, filled the flat screen. He kept seeing the smiling eyes of the boy who'd hummed the ballad. They'd been waiting for him, hadn't they? He stood, walked to the kitchen and back. He was not sure what to do. He sat there, watching the phone in his hand, waiting. He thought he heard ringing in his ears, then couldn't be sure and didn't want to think about it. A throb persisted in his head anyway.

After a while, he went upstairs to his bedroom and lay down. He placed his phone on his stomach and, glancing at a row of shelved books, tried to think of something that might occupy his mind.

In the morning, she still did not answer. Thoughts filled Seth's mind. He made excuses and discarded them just as fast. None of it made sense. Doubt raced his heart, and he felt his mind working very fast. He stayed by the phone, checking, checking, checking.

Before he started up the Navigator, he removed a nine iron from his father's golf bag and laid it in the front seat beside him.

At her grandmother's he pounded the door. Silence. He thought of going back to the car. A dog came on, a sort of hound with a squarish head and a boxy muzzle; it ambled steadily up the street in a deranged sidewise trot, looking straight ahead, pensive, and then was gone. The block was quiet. He saw a curtain fall back into place and knocked again, harder. The door swung open and she stood icily.

"What?" Her face was a cold, unfeeling glaze.

Seth was breathing hard. "You wanna tell me what's happening here?"

"Hey, it's whatever round here, Navy Boy."

Seth's shoulders sank and his head sagged. "That's what this is about?"

"I guess you ain't taking me to the prom?"

"What prom?"

"Any prom." Her arms were crossed.

Seth stood, squint-eyed.

"You must've known this all along," she said.

But Seth wasn't thinking about that yet. "I might go in the Navy"—

—"ain't no *might*. I know what I saw."

"So you—you set me up?"

"Barely." She paused, then added grudgingly. "They weren't supposed to hurt no one."

He touched his head absently where the skin had already tightened. "And I'm gonna find those fools too," he said.

"I'd leave that alone."

Seth watched her. Her coldness made her a stranger. "I don't even know you right now," he said.

"I don't know you, either. *And* you a damn lie. No different than the rest of the world: just out for yourself."

Her eyes were glassy and pink, and he began to ache for his own stupidity. He cast about in his mind for some explanation—as much for himself as for her. Why had he made a secret out of something she had a right to know? Why hadn't he thought of *her* feelings in all this? An image rose in Seth's mind of someone whose courage had failed. For a moment he thought of telling her to pack her bags. They'd hit the road right now and the Navy could kick rocks, but all he said was, "You're wrong about that."

"Well it's almost June. The date said June. So when was it exactly that you were gonna tell me? 'Cause I'm thinking you weren't. Or maybe you were just killing time till then?"

"Don't say that. You know that's not true."

"You weren't going to tell me, were you?" she said. "You were just gonna bounce. One day you'd just be—*poof*—gone."

"I was gonna tell you," he said. "I was."

She shook her head. "You sure enough got a roundabout way of doing it."

"I haven't even told my parents."

"You ain't been laying in your parents' bed."

He dropped his eyes. Below her beige cargo shorts, her feet were bare and her nails were painted a fiery red and looked pretty.

She glanced away. "I betcha everyone else knows. Your friends or whatever."

"No one else knows. I swear it."

She seemed to gulp air. "You live in a place where people worry about who's going through their garbage, or whose towel is more absorbent. You the ones they made the commercial for. Soufflé people with invisible fences and dinner napkins folded into birds. That ain't me. It was stupid to think it was gonna be me."

They watched each other. He moved forward to hold her, but her shoulders shied back. "Don't."

He froze and took a slow step back. His hands hung loosely at his sides. "This is crazy."

"Is it?"

"Yes," he said. "Yes, it is."

She drew a long breath. "It's not even really safe for you here," she said. "Not right now anyway."

"I ain't scared of them." But his eyes misgave him and he turned and swept his gaze down the block.

She inched closer and stared hard at the crown of his head, now a little afraid of what she might find. "Where did it happen?" she asked.

"What?"

"Where did they hurt you?"

"They didn't," he said, but she had already seen where the scabbed hair tufted like a fallen leaf behind his ear.

A heave went through her chest. She sat down on the steps,

brought a balled Kleenex to her nose and held it there. "Boy, oh boy. I made a big mistake falling in love with you. My people warned me. They're real good at spotting liars, hoodlums, bluffers, fiends, bad apples, et cetera. They told me: watch it. Just 'cause he's experimenting don't make him Gandhi."

Her anger was spent now, and her eyes looked dull and remote.

"I thought you were different." Her voice sounded puzzled. "I told people so."

"Stop," he said, closing his eyes.

Inside, where her belly was in knots, she wanted to find a way to let this slide, to let it be okay, but knew she couldn't.

He said, "Listen, I'm a bonehead. I know it. The biggest you've ever seen. But I'm crazy about you."

"Yeah, what you gonna do now? Tell the United States Navy you changed your mind? Call it off? I gotta girl now?"

For a long while neither said anything.

She was picking at the short blades of grass that sprouted between the concrete steps. "I been up all night. Thinking. Thinking about everything. I was afraid—I still am. I don't even know what of." She seemed to be concentrating. "You even had my grandmother up, checking on me. This morning, she came into my room and sat down on the bed and said, 'Summer's just around the corner. Days getting longer. It's no time to be down.' Then she wrapped me up tight like she was gonna hug the hurt out of me."

They were quiet.

"The summer doesn't feel close now, does it?" she asked.

"I don't know," he said.

Across the street some little girls came out and began chalking out hopscotch boxes on the sidewalk.

"You gotta move with the world or get run over, right?" she said, more to herself.

He was flicking away a tear. In her head, she was practicing—she could hear herself—practicing how it would be, almost spelling the sounds of the words she needed, coaxing herself through it, so that the feeling would come out steady and real, and not the broken sobs of some bawling chump, until she heard herself drawing a breath, pushing out those last hard words: *Goodbye, Seth. Be careful over there.*

Colors make loops inside of loops. I listen to the clothes in falling circles, losing their weight. Laundry soap sweetens the air. I'm trying to see Cara's face, but she's all over, doing her work. She trails a mesh cart to the washers. Her arms are full of strangers' clothes. She always looks good: little skirt, shiny vest. Her eyes get brighter little by little if you watch them.

"You know I don't have a lot of time," I say. "He's gonna be up there waiting on me."

"I'll be off soon," Cara says. "An hour at most."

"You make me late."

A dryer stops. She goes to it. "I wish we had the night."

"We'd walk over to the park. Find a bench near the fountain. Tilt back. You don't have to live here to know that."

"I'd pick the music," she said. "And it wouldn't be any of that whack house music you keep bumping."

"I'd tell you a story. And hope for a breeze."

"I'd make you feel at home."

"You're the prettiest girl I know around here, Cara."

"I'm the only girl you know around here, James."

"Maybe I've met some others. 'Cause I'm girl crazy. And you've seen me make friends."

"You better don't," she said.

"All right. You're the prettiest girl anywhere."

"That's more like it."

"Do you think I'm floating? I feel like I'm floating," I say. "It must be the heat."

"You do all that crazy walking. You know there are buses."

If you walked past me and Cara you might think I live in this city. Maybe you've seen me here before and that's what you think, that this is where I clean my clothes, in a neighborhood that's always been mine. I've got a ticket stub in my pocket from a movie I went to with Cara because I visit here three days a week and I always see Cara, but if you asked who put me on this blind errand it wouldn't have anything to do with Cara or laundry or this neighborhood either.

Mama bought me a flip phone to keep time. Then they excused me early for the school year and I started hearing things harder to sort out than the International Date Line or isosceles triangles or anything else from school. I never forget any of what's said about my brother Kitson, but I lose track sometimes and ask questions to stay with it.

First thing in the morning Mama was flapping our covers with a prayer under her breath and I didn't know if I was supposed to get up or kneel and in no time me and Kitson were on that train from 30th Street Philadelphia to Baltimore, blinking away the sun between the shadows. While Mama went on to work, I took little Kitson where I was told. I've been on a Philly local before, but I never rode a train all the way to Baltimore. At first, before we learned our way, I'd be on that train still hearing Mama's directions and names and appointments and times all spilling together—Dr. Madison on Jefferson? Or Dr. Jefferson on Madison?

Inside Johns Hopkins everybody's a doctor. Glassed-in labs, with a guard that stays to one side of the door too—like I'd want anything with his germy beakers. I hold my breath when I pass that lab. The buildings go on forever, everything shut-in under lights that shine the same day or night. The white hallways and scrubbed tile floors always gonna look new.

Take this elevator to that corridor to get this test. Different doctor behind every wall. There. Not there. Some kind of gameland. Door flies open, three more pop out. Started thinking: these hitters don't go home. Doctors got their own beds. Underground somewhere. Sleep in white coats. Wake up. Pump up one those stills. See who's here. See what's what. See who we can snatch up and plug into what's called an infusion pump. Kitson could show you the bruise the needle spreads over the top of his chest.

Kitson's their research. That's why he doesn't have one doctor but a roomful. The doctors pay for our train and, if Kitson's got his appetite, we eat three-dollar sweet buns from the café car. The doctors get to try their medicine on Kitson and solve everything. Charts and folders pile up in their laps. These doctors have the perfectest teeth and cabbage-white faces like they've all been gassed by the same crazy dream.

First week me and Kitson were in a little examining room with so many doctors at once there was hardly room for any of us. One of the doctors tapped up and down on Kitson's spine and said something I didn't catch to another doctor. I said, "It seems like you've got a lot of it figured out."

Doctor said, "Medicine? Yes sir, James. We give 'em hell here. I wish I understood my pension half as good. Tax man takes all those tamales and I can't even call him a cheat."

Pretty soon doctors were talking to us from all directions so I said, "Kitson looks fine to me."

Doctor said, "We'll probably end up spoiling most of Kitson's summer."

Doctor said, "We'll administer a combination of drugs."

Doctor said, "You really can't finesse a disease like this."

Doctor said, "The girls will be falling all over Kitson again soon enough."

I said, "It must be nice being able to, you know, fix people up."

They take all day with Kitson. After a few days I didn't feel bad about not waiting through the morning and afternoon because I can't keep still all that time. I didn't know this place so I was out in the watery heat with my shirt balled up in my hand, the sun like a fire cape on my back, walking and walking and walking. Pretty soon the blocks ran out of fancy hospital and sprinklers flicking over red and yellow flower beds, and the men weren't wearing dress slacks and the women weren't in heels and Baltimore looked just like Philly: old and raggedy.

Those first days I walked all the way to Mt. Vernon, where dudes thought I was queer or a junkie on his game and I watched the pigeons and let them wonder. I rested in a laundromat with two giant, humming fans where there was no one to yap at me but people with clothes baskets and they were busy matching socks or talking back to the game show on TV. I sat there in the laundromat, glad to be out from under that flame-thrower up in the sky, arms perched up on the seat backs, hoping they don't make Kitson feel any worse than he already does.

I had all these things on my mind when this girl snapped her fingers in my eyes and said, "You're so quiet. Dryers put you in a trance?"

I looked up. "Probably so," I said, and I was talking to Cara. She was cleaning lint traps. Sweat glistened on her pretty cheeks.

I checked my new phone, showing off. I had an hour to spit some game before I had to start back for Kitson.

Me and Kitson, feeling the train's weight riding that line, looking out the window, rolling back home to Philly: spidered glass on dark factories, chrome-rusted fenders piled in ditch water and beyond the swept-back brush a man sits on a back porch, elbows on his knees. Empty boxcar freights in a train yard, a boarded-up savings and loan, people at a lunch counter so close we can see the gas jet rising off the stove. A woman holding a child while he feeds a coin into a parking meter, giggling like he won something. Near a heap of oil drums a yellow dog sleeps on his belly. The blue neon of a dancer's hips tip one way and then the other, the sign flashing, *Refreshments*. It's all coming and going, slipping off like a long mural. And Kitson would be chewing his gum, headphones on over his Phillies baseball cap, turning the pages of his *Guinness Book of World Records*, and after a bit he shivers into sleep, the book in his lap. Lots of times I stretched out my legs and thought about the doctor who said we're going to be optimists. When we came to Philly, I gave Kitson a little shake.

Last week, a rainy morning, and Kitson climbed onto my back and we made a breakaway tear down a ramp for the grounds outside. The drizzle pulled the gray sky with it and we stomped up the puddles on a deserted patio. Later that day, after the rain was gone and the sun was a hard dot yellow rushing through the blue and after the nurse had let her machine fly and clocked Kitson's pulse and wrote it into his file and moved off, I asked Kitson if he was ready for another chicken run and Kitson eased back into his pillows and kept real still and said, "James, what is gravity?" And so, using the moon and astronauts and how they jump higher than anyone at the playground if they want, I explained what I thought gravity was, because I wasn't exactly sure myself, and Kitson said it felt like he might have fallen through his gravity.

At the pool in Patterson Park I follow Cara's bare feet over the pavement. Her toes are long and angular, like segments of twig. She wears a gold ankle bracelet into the pool. I'm standing in water up to my waist. Cara's got powerful legs. She swims out to the deep end, kicking her way across the top of the water, back and forth, like she can't help that she's got water wings. When she comes back to me, I tell her.

"I can't swim, Cara."

She brushes water off her face. "You're making it up."

I shake my head.

"I'll teach you. It's easy. You'll see."

"I'm good. I'll just watch you."

"You can't just stand here." She slaps water at my head. The water stings my eyes, and I turn away.

"I'm telling you, you'll pick it right up. It's cinchy. Ready? On three."

She pulls my wrists. I like the bouncy lightness of my feet in the water, the drag on my knees. We inch in deeper and I'm holding Cara's wet hands for dear life.

When I get back up there, Kitson's been moved to a different ward where he can stay overnight. I have to look at *Time* magazine before I can see him. They won't let Kitson come home, and he's not ready for any more medicine right now so they're giving him time to rest. In his room I finish the magazine. Then I get right up to the TV and drop the volume real low and start to feeling bad for ever accusing Kitson of visiting the school nurse just for the apple juice. When Kitson wakes up, I tell him, no train ride for him tonight. He's not awake too long before he dozes off again. I almost go back down to see Cara but I'll be late tonight and Mama will worry so instead I take my transportation voucher for Penn Station. On the train I hold onto the seat tops as I pass through the cars.

I smell my shoulder. Mama's going to ask why I smell like chlorine, especially my hair. She wouldn't believe her eyes if she saw me kicking through the water the way Cara showed me. In a field older kids play baseball under lights. The outfielders seem caught in place under the yellow beams, like lifting their feet might splinter the light they're in. I watch the uniforms before they pass out of view. The glow from the baseball field drifts into the sky.

The conductor told me how the train goes all the way to New England where the Red Sox play in Fenway Park. A map in the car lays out the route, right along the coast. I'm sure there is a lot to see up there, and I don't think we'd have any trouble finding our way. Maybe call Cara, get her to come with us. I know Kitson would like her.

The kids outside had been calling him White Boy because of his father, and Jess had stayed in his room all day playing Madden.

His father could be loud, and Tommy was loud now, hollering from the living room. "You can't hide inside."

Jess came out.

His father looked over the column of cards he'd dealt himself. "You can't hide inside," he said again. "Not in my house you can't."

"They don't bother me," Jess said.

"You keep acting like a shut-in, they gonna think they did."

"I'm not," Jess said.

His eyes lingered on the boy. "I got a taste for Twinkies something terrible." He raised two singles.

"But two dollars isn't"—

"Keep questioning me, Jess. See if you don't cry like an onion." His father pinched a wad of cheddar from the bag and seated it on a salt cracker.

Just then his sister came downstairs.

Seneca was seven years older than Jess. She had ringlets of dark hair, which tufted above the shoulders and black frame glasses. If she'd ever been afraid of anything, Jess had never seen it. Sockless in white Chucks, she'd already changed into her black leotard and stirruped, gray tights. Into her purse, she threw satin-pink pointe shoes, ear buds, keys, Carmex, and a tube of sunflower seeds.

Two months ago, their mother had gone into Johns Hopkins, slept and never woke.

Now they were here, at their father's.

In the hall, Jess lifted a knee and tugged on one red Puma.

Tommy regarded his daughter. "You getting a little high on yourself, don't you think?"

Jess listened. He could hear his father working up to something.

"Hey, Seneca." Tommy paused, jimmying a toothpick between his teeth. "Before you scoot on out, tell me something."

In the mirror, she straightened her back.

"Is it"—a mocking laugh broke up his words—"is it because them ballerinas can twist their bodies all around that these boys keep calling your phone?"

She faced him, looking her father dead on. "You're not funny."

"You say you're grown. Well, that's grown-woman talk. And it's not cute to go around thinking you're too pretty for a little teasing."

"And you wear people out with your bull."

His mouth turned down. "She's harder than you, Jess."

Jess finished lacing up his Puma and did not answer.

On her way out, Seneca bent to her brother's ear. "Don't talk to that man."

No one knew his real name or where he'd come from. To the kids around Carey Street, he was Wizzur. And although he had not been there when Jess entered the store, Wizzur was in the pooling shade when Jess came out. He wore the same tweed jacket Jess had seen before. His grimy dress corduroys were looped with a terry-cloth sash. Some kids believed he had an invisible hand and gave him a few coins for it; others sneered at Wizzur, calling him Sewer Rat or Dukey Breath.

Wizzur eyed the Twinkies. "I'm a fool for sweets."

Jess stopped. Wizzur's face was knobby and raw—white like his father's—and his gray hair was vaselined over his ears and hung straight below.

A boy on a bicycle coasted in, circling. "Watch his hands, White Boy," he warned. "He got sleeves in his sleeves."

Jess had seen Wizzur vanish quarters in his palm and bend a spoon with his mind. He stared at Wizzur's sleeves. "Is it true you keep your tricks in there?"

Wizzur patted one arm, then the other. "And beehives for my honey?"

Jess hid a smile. "Then why do you rub an elbow before it happen?"

Wizzur withdrew from his jacket an empty Land of Lakes butter carton. "I'm certain you've never seen breasts like hers."

Jess looked at the Indian woman on the box. "Someone said you can open locks just by listening to them."

"I'd be in the CIA if I could." He clicked a fingernail on the box. "Look it. The lady I'm talking about is before us now. Not up anybody's sleeve, or in anybody's safe."

The boy on the bike yanked up the handlebars, pulling it into a wheelie—"his face stink"—and pedaled away.

"Where my Hostess?" Tommy squatted beside his Buick Riviera, working a rag between the spoked rims.

Jess stiffened.

"C'mon now," Tommy said. "Me and Mr. Raj want a Twinkie." He winked at their neighbor, Raj, who clasped one wrist behind his back and looked down.

"I don't have them," Jess said.

Tommy had buffed the rim to a high gloss, and still he worked at it. "Why is that?"

Jess looked at father's flattop, hay-colored and glossy with sweat where it was squared off.

"I'ma ask you one more time," Tommy warned. "Why is that, J?"

Jess hesitated, started, stopped, gathered himself and said it outright. "I gave 'em away."

Tommy stopped buffing and looked up. "You did what now?"

"I gave 'em away." Then not hearing himself, Jess said it again, "I gave 'em away."

Tommy balled the rag in his fist. "Now, why would you do that?"

"He looked bad. Like he ain't have nothing to eat."

"Who's that?"

"That man that always be out there," Jess said. "The one that go by Wizzur."

"Call hisself what?"

"It's 'cause he act like a wizard or something."

Tommy hung his head. "As many years as I been here, and not nary a word about wizards." He looked up. "But you found one."

"Oh," Jess clarified. "He's a bummy man now. Like a homeless."

Tommy took his time getting up, draping the rag neatly over the edge of the pail. "So a wizard got my Twinkies? That's what you telling me?"

"He does do magic."

Tommy dried his hands on his jeans.

"He got stuff under his sleeves, supposedly. Like twine or different bottle caps"—

At once Tommy snatched a handful of Jess' shirt and yoked him up. Air fluttered under the boy's feet, and his sneakers scrabbled for pavement. Tommy sunk his forehead against his son's. "He's gonna have to find his own."

Jess turned from the sour fog of cheese and crackers. "I"—

"You a lie." Tommy set him down and turned his shoulders. "And you better hotfoot it back there and get mine."

Jess moved on, head bowed.

"Go easy," Raj said.

"It's for his own good." Tommy flicked his smarting fingers. "His mother put them in those county schools and now he's giving away my money like a Red Cross."

As Jess went along, he passed a fenced lot of flatbed trucks. He let his fingers drag the metal lattice, pinging. He thought of something Seneca told him—*some people steal 'cause they have no other way.* He had not stolen before because he had not had to, but if the Twinkies had been eaten or if Wizzur was gone, he would have no other way.

Jess found Wizzur where he had left him. He saw the Twinkies on the store's brick sill. An air conditioner whirred, trickling a stream on the pavement.

"My father say you can't have our Twinkies. I gotta bring 'em back."

One eye squinted. "The transaction is over. These are mine."

"My father say"—

"He'll have to purchase his own." Wizzur took the Twinkies from the sill.

Confusion swam in Jess' face. He looked at the gaps where Wizzur's teeth were missing. "He did," Jess said. "That was his money that paid for them."

"Your father is not anybody to me. And I don't owe him anything."

Jess realized he would have to get in close and take them. He stepped forward, mulling the angles. Wizzur was frail, but he was ready to protect what little he had. He spread his feet, lifted his cane and jabbed it, harpoon-like, at Jess' face.

The sidewalk took a cock-eyed jolt and leveled again. Jess' legs held. He straightened and touched the back of his fingers to his mouth. Red smeared his knuckles. His tongue searched the wound, and he turned for home.

"Take me to him," his father said. "Show me."

He walked purposively, and Jess fell in behind. "Look at that pigeon." Tommy pointed. "See how that bird is hopping 'round? He got his eye out for something. A peck here, a peck there, but he's watching his back. You think that pigeon just gonna let somebody take him off? This ain't no okey doke. This ain't no *la dee da*. You ain't in the county no more."

They came to the store.

Wizzur had moved on, but he had not gotten far. At the next block, he shuffled one hip and then the other, favoring his left, as if keeping certain loose parts together, his cane wobbling with the work. They caught up to him crossing the street, still holding the Twinkies. Tommy came on in a sprightly, loping stride and swept out the indigent's legs, dropping him cleanly. The cane clattered away.

Wizzur lay on a storm grate where leaves and plastic bags had crusted. His hips bucked once, one hand pinned to his tailbone, and fell back again. Tommy reached for the Twinkies and when Wizzur clutched them tighter, Tommy backed up—"You mash my Twinkies, I'ma mash you"—and measured out another, his toes digging into Wizzur's ribs.

Jess moved in, caught his father's elbow, softly at first, and then, more firmly.

His father whirled, an open hand raised to strike. "I'ma be the one who say when."

"Don't," Jess said. "Don't do anymore."

Tommy glared, his brows snagged in disgust. He spat and turned away.

On the ground, Wizzur had folded in on himself. Tommy dipped into the crook of his arm, and this time, the Twinkies came free easily.

His father looked down and wagged his head. "How you think it gonna end, Chief, ain't necessarily how it do." He propped a foot on the base of a light post and smoothed a scuff on his Nike. "He ain't even that old—just a drunk that never took care of hisself."

Wizzur's chest heaved and his arms settled at his sides.

"He gonna need some help," Jess said.

"He's gonna have to help himself."

"We can call him an ambulance."

"He can get it his own self."

"But he can't."

Tommy peeled away the plastic wrapper and bit into a Twinkie. "He can if he wants it bad enough. Hospital's open all night."

Jess looked at his father. "But"—

—"It's on him if he's gonna do for himself." Clods of yellow cake and white crème blinked in his father's mouth.

Then his father wheeled and started back. "Keep up now, Jess."

Jess glanced at his father's bopping shoulders and then his eyes fell again to the ground. He picked up Wizzur's cane and brought it to him. "Here," Jess said. "I got your cane, Mister."

Wizzur's eyes were turned up and seemed to look through the boy.

Jess looked around. His gums, where Wizzur had struck him, throbbed. He realized how strange it looked, standing over an old man in the gutter. Porch spindles ran in bunches up the street, but the porches were empty. At the far end of the block, tree roots had pitched up the sidewalk and some kids took turns on a skateboard. Across the street, a fence was kinked green with ivy and Jess could hear voices behind it.

Jess knelt and turned an ear, bending closer, listening. "You might just need to lay up for a little."

Then he thought if he kept talking, it would help Wizzur come around so that his eyes would start seeing what they were looking at again.

"You got a lot of good tricks. Probably got a bunch you never even shown." He paused. "And I know it must feel good the way you do magic."

He tugged lightly at the man's arm. "It's not good to lie in the street like this, all alone."

Jess laid his cheek on the street and lifted the cuff on the man's jacket sleeve, peering into the dark to see if what the boy on the bike had said was true.

A weak breeze rose and fell.

Then, because grown-ups were always asking, he began to tell about school. "My teacher says there's lava sloshing around under us, but I think we'd have felt it. My school now, it's way older than my last one. One pipe, well in the boys' room anyway, it's always knocking, and they keep a pile of cat litter under it. And my classroom's got two speakers—up high on the wall with cloth on them? —that when the principal says his announcements, it just comes out like he's crumpling bags."

A blackened banana peel and a crushed Castrol Motor Oil jug lay near Wizzur's neck. Jess stood and toed them away. Then he saw that Wizzur had wet himself.

"Oh," Jess said and looked away.

For a while he couldn't think of anything to say. Wizzur's breathing was loud, like a catch had gotten in it. Jess sat on his heels. "My father—Seneca says something wrong with him, and that's how come he's not sorry for how he acts."

Kneeling there, he looked at the man more closely. The tip of each big toe curled up, nosing through the leather tops of his dusty loafers. A triangle of torn fabric flapped off one knee. Some of his grey hair had gotten into his ears, and Jess saw how ashen and stringy his neck was under the jawbone.

No one ever slept with their eyes open that he'd seen. He wondered what Wizzur was thinking.

Sirens sounded in the distance. Jess turned to it. He looked at Wizzur and swung back to the sound again.

He stood and brushed off his knees, backing away. Then he turned and moved off, picking up his feet. He crossed one street and then another, his Pumas beating the sidewalk beneath him. His lungs stung and in his gasps Jess heard the wheezy hiss of Wizzur fighting for air.

His name was Dario. He came into class and slipped between a row of desks, like he wasn't hauling a load of grief. He was nineteen—tall, bean-thin, vigilant eyes, patchy beard. The buttons on his pink Polo dress shirt were fastened to the neck. He set a foil-wrapped pizza slice on the desk. "I'm gonna have to leave early," he said. "I got a funeral to go to."

I stopped passing out worksheets. "Oh," I said cautiously. "I'm sorry."

He was quiet.

"Was it someone close to you?" I asked.

"My brother."

He could've been talking about the weather. That's how he said it. But with those two words the room changed. Some gloomy alchemy of empathy and helplessness fell upon the class: seventeen city kids and me, their U.S. History teacher. In our uneasy stillness an implicit promise went up: we would listen.

"Oh, man," I said softly. "I'm sorry."

Funerals were not uncommon at our school. Each year, students were shot in their neighborhood or someone else's. Some years it was one or two that died, sometimes more. It was never zero. Many of these students had inhabited the world so vividly that, years after they've left it, the mind still rebels against the facts of their deaths. Here, in the middle of my career, I could fill a classroom with these incandescent souls.

The first was Vincent, whose cramped, cursive script filled his essays with carefully organized thoughts. In the late 1990s, Vincent delighted in the music of Juvenile and the pronunciation of Slobodan Milosevic. Under slightly better circumstances, he'd probably have gone on to a first-rate college. Then I'd have fewer reasons to think of him. But his solid academic skills were of limited use in West Baltimore, and after a while his school attendance became irregular and his class work gradually took on signs of indifference and he was shot on the same street where he'd lived most of his life. I never learned why, only that his friends sped him to the doors of Shock Trauma and fled. Over the years, I'd come to understand that such murders occurred over disagreements many people would regard as trivial, but the violence was almost never random. Vincent had been a perceptive and sensitive kid, and I have wondered whether he knew his life was in jeopardy.

More than a year after Vincent's murder, I got a call from Sanae, a former student who had been a friend and classmate of Vincent's. She had by then graduated and was working at a Walgreens. She asked if I could take her to the cemetery in Lansdowne. She both needed a ride and didn't want to visit Vincent's grave alone. I really didn't want to go, but I agreed.

The grounds of this cemetery were untended, the narrow asphalt lane pitched and frayed. We parked and began wandering around, looking for Vincent under the broiling July sun. Wooden stakes, upon which were the scrawled names of the dead, greatly outnumbered headstones. The rows of stakes were everywhere, some broken, some flattened under a tangle of grass, some whose names were completely faded. Dripping sweat, we walked the grounds, tearing at the weeds and tall switch grass, vainly searching for Vincent. After a while, it began to feel hopeless. Ahead of us, a platoon of stakes capped a gentle hill and banked away. Still, we kept on, searching. Eventually, we spotted a lone groundskeeper, sheltering under a shady tree. He rose, sloth-like, put on his sun-hat and walked us to Vincent.

Afterwards, Sanae and I went to a Ruby Tuesday's and, over hamburgers, talked about Vincent and other kids from those years who'd *gotten got*. Kenneth, who went out of his way not to get mixed up in anything, resisted a stick-up boy, and in an instant was gone. TJ, an introspective hardhead who created ribald box cartoons that showed the folly of youth, fought another young man, won, and then died on his own front steps when the rival returned that same night strapped with a sawed-off. Trey, whose fingers and palms coaxed slick beats from the desk tops, got into a neighborhood beef that ended with his body in a dumpster not three blocks from school.

Now, I regarded Dario, sitting in the back of my classroom, and again offered a muffled apology.

We were waiting—all of us waiting—for somebody to show that we had heard Dario and that we understood, or for Dario to say more.

"Are you okay?" I asked.

He lowered his head and stroked his hair forward. "I can't call it."

And then you saw it—on his face a glaze of sorrow so deep he looked utterly bereft.

We waited.

"That was my little brother." His voice trailed off, and he made an effort to swallow.

I took a seat.

"I've been up all night," he said. "Keep hearing his voice."

Some students had turned towards him; others had not budged, reluctant, perhaps, to get too close. A few held their faces low, chins dipped almost to their chests.

"We gonna fight," Dario went on. "Best believe that. When I see him, we gonna scrap. He ain't even supposed to be out there. He don't bang like that. That's not him. Should've kept hisself in school. Instead, his dumb ass go and get himself killed." He clasped his hands behind his head. "Yeah, we gonna fight."

It was October. Fall was coming on, a chill in the sky. Outside, in the alley, leaves and trash eddied in the wind.

"I wish there was something I could say, Dario," I said. "Something wise or helpful or soothing."

"You can't say nothing, Mr. Lima." He sounded like he felt bad for me.

I picked up the box of Kleenex from my desk and walked it over to him, grateful to be able to offer this small gesture. But at once Dario set it aside on the window sill.

Kevin capped his juice bottle. "Man, I don't know what I'd do. You doing better than me, bro. If that'd happened—I'd be so torn up I'd be going crazy."

"That's how it be out here." Brandon was a prickly boy, a sullen clock-watcher given to sulks, and he was scolding us for forgetting.

Dario cut his eyes at him. "Nah, man. This don't make no sense. It was over something petty."

"That's what I'm saying," Brandon went on. "It be the littlest thing. But you get the wrong one toting that steel?" He wagged his head. "Man, people get killed for stupid stuff nowadays. It's either somebody think they gonna run your pockets or girls or"—

—"This man knows that." Teresa locked eyes with Brandon. "This really not the time."

"You all tryna sit here and act like we're not living this every day," Brandon said.

"That's not what we're saying." Teresa smacked her gum.

"Alright, Yo." Brandon shook his head, aggrieved, his thumb working the clicker on his pen.

Derrick, a big kid heading to Del State on a football scholarship, checked him. "Chill, bruh."

Brandon blew into his cupped hands, stood, went to the window, cranked it open, and spat. Ordinarily, I'd have told him to use the men's room for that. This morning, I said nothing and only watched. I thought he might leave, but he sat again.

Dario stared at the ground. "I ain't mad. He's just speaking the truth." He looked at the wrapped pizza slice, as if suddenly remembering it. He peeled back the foil; the cheese glistened and the foil was streaked with oil and red sauce.

"I can't eat this," Dario said. "My man's went and got it for me when I came out the house. He said 'you gonna need something on your stomach.' And he went in the carry-out and got that for me. But I can't eat this." He turned to Alford, the student closest to him. "Yo, you want this, Yo?"

Alford wore glasses and a linty pea coat, which he drew tighter around him. "No. I brought my lunch," he said apologetically.

Dario held it up. "Anyone want this pizza?"

Silence.

He set it on the desk, creased the foil closed and drew a long breath.

I looked at him. He looked rough, like he'd been out there a while, years maybe, grinding and chasing a dollar anyway he could. And you wondered how it would ever get better for him.

"I can't even be around my family. They keep getting all mushy. I mean crying till they got snot coming out of their nose. All that carrying on—I can't do it."

Derrick spoke again: "You gotta cry sometimes. You gotta let that out."

"I don't know." Dario squinted, his face full of questions. "It supposed to do something, but what it do?"

A chair scraped the floor. Through the slatted blinds, bands of sunlight fell across the room.

Wesley was in class that day and he asked, "What's your brother's name?"

"Minta," Dario said. "We call him Minta. When he was little, he couldn't never say *mint* right. My aunt, my Mom, they thought it was funny and it just stuck. He still that way—adding on to words and whatnot, playing with them."

Wesley nodded.

"Feel like I'ma get home and he's gonna be hiding in the closet," Dario said. "Laughing at how he got us trippin'. Minta's always got jokes, and that'd be just like him. Pop out with my nephew's light saber and surprise everybody. He be taking shit too far. I'm telling you. He extra."

Marcel, who often entered the room already in mid-rap, joyously taking us through another of his rhymes, had not said anything yet.

Now he swiveled his chair to face Dario. "You alright, Yo?" Worry pinched his eyes, and a plaintive concern thinned his voice.

Dario did not answer and Marcel repeated the questions. "You alright? You good?"

A small shrug went through Dario's shoulders, and Marcel went on. His questions grew louder—"You alright? You good?"—then softened again as he turned them into statements of assurance. "You got this, Yo. You're alright."

We watched him.

Marcel was a dreamy pencil-chewer with neat close hair, and slender arms to go with his slender shoulders, and it was as if having started, he could no longer stop. He set his elbows on his knees and smiled a strange smile, his words stretching to a plea. "C'mon, D. You're good, Yo. You gonna be alright. *C'mon.*"

Irritation flickered in Dario's eyes and cleared. "I'm alright. I'ma handle this."

Marcel fought something in himself, looked like he might start again, and gave it up. His pleas fell away, and it was quiet then. Teresa stopped chewing her gum and watched him. Derrick turned one of the twists that styled his hair. Brandon made eraser crumbs on his desk. Kevin peeled at the label on his juice bottle. Alford's hands remained sunk in his pea coat. The other kids were quiet, thinking their thoughts. And there was only the silence of our mourning.

ACKNOWLEDGMENTS:

Thank you to my dear friend Mary Clark who listened to most of these stories during weekly No Big Deals and whose expert insights improved every one of them. Her belief in my work never faltered and has buoyed me when I needed it most.

Thank you to the many students who've allowed me into their lives and whose warmth, depth and courage have been a well of inspiration to me.

Thank you to Joe, David, Neil, Maxine, Katy, Jeff, Lia, Zachary, Jake, Sara, Harper, Carol, Steve, Peter, Audrey, Eli—I am grateful for all the support. And special thanks to Madeline whose enduring faith in my work has been invaluable.

Thank you to Maks who has improved my life immeasurably.

And thank you to Kathleen Wheaton, Robert Williams, Clair Lamb, Nathan Leslie, Barbara Shaw and Patricia Schultheis for their thoughtful and sharp-eyed editing.

9 781941 551233